PRAISE FOR
The Archive of Feelings

"Affecting...Stamm delivers a striking and earnest conclusion. Fans of the author will love this efficient and wistful work." —*Publishers Weekly*

"[Stamm] continually presents his readers with captivating works...beautiful." —*Literaturkritik*

"A haunting text about loneliness." —*Südwest Presse*

PRAISE FOR
Peter Stamm

"One of Europe's most exciting writers...Stamm's talent is palpable, but what makes him a writer to read, and read often, is the way he renders contemporary life as a series of ruptures. Never entirely sure of their position, his characters engage in a constant effort to establish their equilibrium." —*New York Times Book Review*

"Peter Stamm is an extraordinary author who can make the ordinary absolutely electrifying...Hard to recommend too highly." —Tim Parks

"Excellent...this amorphous tale folds in on itself, becoming a meditation on how memory can distort reality...Fans of Julian Barnes will love this."   —*Publishers Weekly*

"Haunting...The fascinating overall effect of *Indifference* makes it a worthy inclusion among Stamm's other compelling novels."   —*Literary Review*

"There's a satisfying tension between the complexity of the novel's conceit and the simplicity of the writing...lively and well-paced, fully capturing the rhythm of two people walking and speaking...it's a novel about a writer and about people talking, which, in its distortions, takes on larger questions of storytelling and memory."
—*Los Angeles Review of Books*

"*The Sweet Indifference of the World* explores questions of time, identity, and art in prose that is dreamy, melancholic, and beautiful."   —*Book Riot*

"Adroitly translated by the award-winning Hofmann, [Stamm] explores the timeless doppelgänger phenomenon through dual couples whose fleeting interactions engender intriguing questions about singularity and agency and confirm the impossibility of absolutely sure answers."
—*Booklist*

"An elegant dart of a novel as clear and mesmerizing as an M. C. Escher drawing. I felt both lost and found at once. Peter Stamm is a truly wonderful writer."

—Catherine Lacey, Whiting Award winner, Guggenheim fellow, and author of *Certain American States*, *The Answers*, and *Nobody Is Ever Missing*

PRAISE FOR
It's Getting Dark

"[Stamm's] story collection shows the instability of a world we think we know." —*New York Times*

"Stamm, whose precise, dry prose builds suspense in its very insistence on the quotidian, creates narratives simultaneously ordinary and strange, even uncanny. Atmospherically, these stories recall Arthur Schnitzler, or even Edgar Allan Poe...haunting...beautifully translated, as are all his books, by the remarkable Michael Hofmann."

—*Harper's*

"[Stamm's] powerfully unsettling short-story collection catalogs moments when the familiar shifts into the unknown, when we realize how flimsy our constructed realties really are."

—*Literary Hub*, Most Anticipated Books of the Year

"From an author one critic called 'one of Europe's most exciting writers' come a dozen reflective and somber stories about the tenuousness of reality."

—*Los Angeles Times*

"[These stories] all have a latent uneasiness to them, making the reader turn the pages both quickly and apprehensively...Stamm effectively sustains a dark mood."

—*Publishers Weekly*

"Stamm sketches out painfully realistic stories that slowly but surely reveal their strange, uneasy underbellies."

—*The Millions*, Most Anticipated Books

"Peter Stamm doesn't so much yank the rug out from under the reader as ease it slowly, mesmerizingly away, until we stagger and realize that the world has shifted beneath us. These tales are eerie, menacing delights."

—Caitlin Horrocks, author of
Life Among the Terranauts

"A casual, effortless voice belies the intense structural formality in these stories, which take place on the blurred edge between reality, memory, and dream. Language is wielded subtly, sharply, in masterful hands. *It's Getting Dark* burns like ice."

—Shruti Swamy, author of *The Archer*
and *A House Is a Body*

"Michael Hofmann's translation from the German is cool and precise. *To the Back of Beyond* follows Thomas and Astrid in alternating sections; his give a careful account of his route, procuring provisions, the footpaths, slopes, valleys, and streams, the landscape with its 'thin shreds of mist.' She waits, searches, tries to calm the children. One month after Thomas disappears, there is a twist in the plot. It is masterfully timed...Both of them, it is clear, are in thrall to fantasies—one dreams about slipping the ties of responsibility, the other about seamlessly restoring what has been broken."   —*Harper's Magazine*

"...perceptive...What initially seems a paean to a life free of constraints becomes a keen exploration of the marital bond. Stamm's precise observations of nature and character animate every line as both husband and wife confront 'a future that was not prescribed and that could, with every step, be altered.'"   —*The New Yorker*

"Stamm's writing is taut and economical: every word is carefully chosen, and the deceptively simple style rewards close reading...And by abandoning conventional literary realism, Stamm creates a fertile space to explore human relationships and comment on current affairs...In *To the Back of Beyond* Peter Stamm plays with multiple meanings and eschews traditional literary devices, particularly when it comes to the outcome of Thomas's disappearance."   —*Times Literary Supplement*

"From the opening paragraph, Peter Stamm's *To the Back of Beyond* is mysterious and mesmerizing. Many novels have sprung from the premise of a spouse walking away from a marriage, but Stamm's take is entirely original...The book moves smoothly between his point of view and Astrid's, so skillfully that this inexplicable adventure seems completely plausible...Stamm's pivot halfway through the book is masterful: The story opens up, moving forward and backward in time almost simultaneously. The out-come becomes murky, but Stamm's control never wavers... this strange, lovely book is not a story of loss or grief but a hopeful story of profound love."

—*Minneapolis Star Tribune*

THE ARCHIVE OF FEELINGS

ALSO BY PETER STAMM

NOVELS

Agnes

Unformed Landscape

On a Day Like This

Seven Years

All Days Are Night

To the Back of Beyond

The Sweet Indifference of the World

STORY COLLECTIONS

In Strange Gardens and Other Stories

We're Flying

It's Getting Dark

THE

Archive

OF

Feelings

Peter Stamm

Translated from the German by Michael Hofmann

OTHER PRESS
NEW YORK

Originally published in German as *Das Archiv der Gefühle* in 2021
by S. Fischer Verlag GmbH, Frankfurt am Main

Translation copyright © 2023 Michael Hofmann

We wish to express our appreciation to the Swiss Arts Council Pro Helvetia for
their assistance in the preparation of this translation.

Song lyrics on page 145 from "Dis, quand reviendras-tu?" by
Barbara (Monique Serf), Shai Lowenstein, and Talya Eliav, 1962.

Production editor: Yvonne E. Cárdenas
Text designer: Jennifer Daddio / Bookmark Design & Media Inc.
This book was set in Goudy Old Style by
Alpha Design & Composition of Pittsfield, NH

3 5 7 9 10 8 6 4 2

Library of Congress Cataloging-in-Publication Data
Names: Stamm, Peter, 1963- author. | Hofmann, Michael,
1957 August 25- translator.
Title: The archive of feelings / Peter Stamm ; translated from
the German by Michael Hofmann.
Other titles: Archiv der Gefühle. English
Description: New York : Other Press, [2023]
Identifiers: LCCN 2023012180 (print) | LCCN 2023012181 (ebook) |
ISBN 9781635422757 (paperback) | ISBN 9781635422764 (ebook)
Subjects: LCGFT: Romance fiction. | Psychological fiction. | Novels.
Classification: LCC PT2681.T3234 A8813 2023 (print) |
LCC PT2681.T3234 (ebook) | DDC 833/.92—dc23/eng/20230421
LC record available at https://lccn.loc.gov/2023012180
LC ebook record available at https://lccn.loc.gov/2023012181

THE ARCHIVE OF FEELINGS

There was a bit of rain earlier, now the sky's
just half-clouded-over with tough little clouds
whose rims are picked out in the sunlight. The sun
itself has dropped from sight, disappeared behind
the wooded hills, and the temperature's fallen
correspondingly. The water level in the river is
high, a white foaming backwash forms at the steps,
I can almost feel the power of the moving water
as though it were flowing through me, a powerful,
living stream. A hundred yards upstream, where the
water plunges over the weir, the gurgle has made
way for a loud, full-throated roar. Although *roar* isn't
quite right either, it's a little imprecise in its many
meanings and associations, what doesn't roar, the
river, the rain, the wind. The ether roars. Sounds
of water—I should start a file on them, though I
wonder where it would go in my system. Under
Nature, Physics, or even Music? Sounds, smells, light
phenomena, colors, there's so much missing from
my archive, so much that's never been described,
taken on, computed.

I walked along the path that follows the river
up into the valley. Franziska has joined me, I don't
know where she's sprung from, perhaps she was lured
by the water, as was the case always for both of us.

Suddenly she's walking by my side. She doesn't say anything, she just smiles to me when I look over at her, a sort of roguish smile that I could never quite fathom, which is maybe why I love it so much in her. She nods, as though encouraging me to speak, to act. That causes her hair to tumble down across her face, and she brushes it back. I feel like reaching out and touching her neck, kissing it. I love you, I say. I reach for her hand, but there's nothing there.

Sometimes she appears abruptly like that, without my so much as thinking about her, she accompanies me for a bit, and then she vanishes as quickly as she arrives, and I'm on my own.

How long have I been walking? Half an hour, an hour? Ahead of me, a black beetle is crossing the path, and I stop to watch it. I wonder what kind he is? There are hundreds of thousands of different insects, and I can hardly name a dozen: ladybirds, May and June bugs, cockroaches, woodlice, millipedes, grasshoppers, bees and wasps, ants, that's about it. There are so many things I don't know.

The milky shades of spring, with the stronger colors of summer already looming, the breeze, which isn't cold, but isn't warm yet, and makes me shiver a little, not cold, a sensation on the surface.

I took the footbridge and walked back on the other side of the river. The path here is wider and less frequented, in a few places the ground is soft, puddles have formed that reflect the electricity cables overhead and the clouds. As I approach the edge of town, the noises get a little louder.

The nameless path I'm walking, the little allotment gardens, some of them already dug in readiness for spring planting, others still in their winter sleep, and a few of them completely neglected, presumably not tended for years, and behind them the railway line, and a little behind that the highway. The roaring of the river, the roaring of the cars and trucks, a high whine, and then a different roaring that sounds metallic and rhythmic, a train just passing. How to itemize and categorize all that?

I'm tired from walking, I'm out of the habit, and so I stopped at a wooden bench below the weir. I sit by the river and am stunned by the fullness of the impressions that flood my senses. It's the feeling of clarity and permeability that you get the first time you leave the house after a long illness, say, still a little woozy, but alert and with keen senses. I close my eyes, and the roaring seems to get louder, there's more water in the river, it's flowing quicker, it's a muddy yellow. The rain is falling more gently now, before finally stopping altogether. I'm shivering in my trunks, with a towel round my shoulders. The cold gives me a keener sense of my body than usual, everything feels both terribly clear and terribly superficial. I have a sense of happiness that feels not much different from unhappiness.

I think about Franziska, who's most likely at home, doing her homework or baking a cake, or doing whatever girls do. We walk part of the way home together. At the big crossing, where our ways part, we often stop and talk for a long time. I wonder what we talked about then? We never seemed to be short of subjects. Then one of us would notice the time and see it was late, and we were keeping our mothers waiting with lunch.

The way home, still with Franziska in my thoughts, her voice in my ear, her laughter, the things she would say and not say. Then the squeak of the garden gate, and the crunch of gravel in the noonday silence. The buzz of the extractor fan, the smells emanating from the kitchen, the sound of the pips through the open window, the one o'clock news, Mother's voice, the clatter of a pan in the kitchen sink.

When there was no afternoon school and I was left to my own devices, I often thought about

Franziska. Or rather, I didn't think about her, she was just there, walking in the woods with me, watching me do whatever I was doing, sitting by the river beside me, throwing pebbles into the water as I was. She tickled my neck with a blade of grass, like a shy caress. Did you know it's not possible to tickle yourself? she says, and runs the blade of grass across her cheek, and smiles at me.

Was I in love with Franziska? All the time at school, there was talk of this boy and that girl, or her and someone else, and these two are inseparable, but what did it mean? My feelings were much bigger and more bewildering than those of childish couples who were over as soon as they had begun. My feelings for Franziska overwhelmed me, when we were together I had the feeling I was in the middle of the world, and there were only the two of us and this moment in time; nothing and no one else, not school, not parents, not pals. But Franziska didn't love me.

I rarely left home that winter, in fact I went out less and less in the time since I lost my job, and since my separation with Anita, which wasn't really a separation as such. I gave up Anita, the same way as I gave up so many things in these past years, and with her maybe my last chance of leading a normal life, the sort of life you are expected to lead. But no one looked to me for anything anymore, and myself least of all, and so over time I became increasingly withdrawn. Some days I only ventured out of doors as far as the mailbox, or to the garden for a breath of fresh air. I do my grocery shopping in a local store once or twice a week, making a point of going at closing time, when I'm unlikely to run into other customers, then I buy one or two items. Each time, I'm grateful to the owner for greeting me as though I were a complete stranger. Whatever the shop doesn't have I can get from catalogs or the Internet, I adore the unpopulated two-dimensional world of online shopping, the pictures of merchandise against a sterile-looking white background, front view, back view, side view, accessories, technical details, your shopping cart.

I go to the bank when I run out of cash, and to the barber when my hair gets too long. I can't remember when I last went to the doctor, but it's been a while.

I spend most of my time poring over the newspapers and magazines I subscribe to, cutting and pasting relevant articles, giving them codes and putting them in the appropriate files, the work I used to be paid for, and which I continue to carry out on my own behalf since my dismissal, because I don't know what else I would do with my time. Even if everyone says the archive is no longer required and was an anachronism in an age of data banks and Internet searches. Why did my bosses have such a hard time then, letting me take the archive? The original decision to junk it was quickly made by some executive, one of those dynamic characters that people like me only got to see from a distance at the annual Christmas party. But when I suggested taking over the archive in its entirety, including the motile shelving, and storing it in my basement, at that the board got suspicious and wouldn't give me a decision for weeks. My immediate boss came with all kinds of objections, it was much too expensive, would my house be able to tolerate the weight of the files, would the fire department even permit such a quantity of paper to be stored in a private dwelling? I had more than enough money and promised to pay for the removal myself. My basement was spacious and had concrete floors that could easily cope with the weight. And the fire department seemed not even to understand what the problem might be. If you knew what people kept in their basements and attics, said the man on the telephone, and laughed. I thought his laugh had an unpleasant note, as though he was making me privy to a dirty secret.

Even after I had overcome my boss's objections, it still took my superiors weeks before they finally agreed to put the paper archive in my hands. A complicated contract was drawn up, all about copyright and confidential information, and I agreed not to use the archive for any commercial purpose nor to sell it. I read the contract through several times word for word, I have always admired contracts, the tiny type, the thin paper, the structure of the paragraphs, and the strangely convoluted legal language that is supposed to anticipate any and all eventualities. I sometimes thought things only began to exist when they were the subject of contracts: a marriage, a job, a house purchase, an inheritance.

The signing of the document was the one and only time I met the board member in question, and I could tell he thought I was a nutcase, which only had the effect of making me still more determined.

People like that have never understood the true point of the archive, they only ever saw expenses, and divided them by the number of search orders, and realized it didn't pay its way. But tell me, what does? The archive not only points to the world, it is a picture of the world and a world in and of its own. And unlike the world, it has an order, where everything has its appointed place, and can with a little practice be quickly found. That is the true point of the archive. To be there and make order.

The installation of the shelving in the basement was carried out by a specialized firm, which dug grooves in the concrete and laid down rails. The deafening sound of drilling filled the house, the dust penetrated the upstairs rooms, a fine mist that showed the rays of sunbeams, the white light of change.

At last the great day came when a van drew up outside my house, and, groaning and swearing, the movers lugged the crates of files into my basement. I was a little alarmed when I saw how many boxes there were, how much material was now mine, and my responsibility. The excitement of the building work and the removal was so great that it took me a few days to get back to normal. Then the installation of the files was like a slow healing process, restoring order, and finally knowing that everything was in its place.

It's a source of joy every time, to find the right place for an event. A natural disaster, a celebrity divorce, a new public building, a plane crash, the current state of the weather, of anything, there is really nothing that doesn't have a place in the system, or for which a place couldn't be found. And when something is fitted into the hierarchy of subjects, it becomes understandable and governable. If everything is equal, the way it is in the Internet, then nothing has any value.

Files on current events, which are often completed and added to on a daily basis, lie on my desk or on the floor of my office; other items are stowed away in the shelving in the basement, until the moment when a subject comes bobbing up to the surface again, and with it its file.

To maintain the archive is a lot of work and calls for great care. A misfiled article is as good as lost forever. I am sure there must be hundreds of such orphaned texts lying in the wrong place. One day, I have determined, I will go through everything to fish them out and refile them in the correct place, but even in summer, in the so-called silly season when there isn't much news, there isn't the time for such a Herculean undertaking.

The amount of work I have to do may be a further reason why I leave the house less and less over time, and the few times I have done so, the more effort and resolve it cost me. In the immediate wake of my dismissal, it may have been embarrassment that kept me from going out in public. I didn't want to be one of those wretched beings that you can tell from a distance are no longer needed for anything, so I stayed home and did my work for myself. Over time, I became habituated to this solitary existence, and by now it's gotten so that I feel most at home in my four walls, in the house I grew up in, and to which I returned after my mother's death. When I am outside, I feel uncertain and somehow compromised; at home I am shielded from the confusion of the continually changing world, which only disturbs me in my thoughts and memories, and my daily routines.

I get up at half past six, shower, read the data on my little weather station, and copy them down in the notebook where my father before me every day wrote down temperature, air pressure, and humidity. I make coffee and work in my office until twelve. For lunch, I will eat a sandwich and listen to the midday news on the radio. I have a little lie-down for half an hour, but by half past one at the latest I'm back at my desk. In the evening I cook for myself, one of a few simple dishes I know how to make, and that my mother used to make. After supper, I open a bottle of wine, take a book down from the shelf, and read until the bottle is empty, and I feel tired enough to sleep. Earlier, I used to listen to music, but that had the effect of making me feel sentimental, and that

was disagreeable to me. Even Fabienne's chansons
would sometimes reduce me to tears.

Is that really true? Franziska laughs. Oh, laugh
all you like. I know it's childish, but when you sing
about your beloved, I imagine it's me that you're
pining for. You're not the only one who does that, she
says, frowning. But I didn't want to do that, I say, so
I stopped listening to music. By now, I love the quiet
in the house, which is only broken by the hum of the
fridge, a dripping tap, the sounds from the street or
beyond. I like the idea of my voice wafting through
your house, says Franziska, it's coming from outside,
it's springtime, someone is playing the radio outside,
a neighbor maybe, or a builder on some scaffolding,
I'm singing about love, and you get all misty. She
laughs. I turn on the radio. The pips come on, hasn't
that been ditched yet? The time is twelve o'clock.
Here is the midday news.

All my days pass off in the same way, workdays,
Sundays, holidays, it makes no odds. Even my own
birthday I'd probably forget, if I didn't get a card
from someone or other suggesting I get in touch.
But I don't, I wouldn't know what to say. There's
nothing happening in my life, and I've never been
interested in exchanging opinions. Who cares what
I think about this or that politician, or my view of

the condition of my country or my city, whether I'm pro or con the elimination of nuclear power plants? Opinions are nothing to do with facts, they're only feelings, and my feelings are of no concern to anyone. My task is collecting and ordering information. Other people can interpret the world, if that's what they want to do.

Maybe I once conceived of a different kind of life for myself or could have managed a different kind of life. I wasn't always a hermit, just my attempts at a normal existence were crowned with failure, that can happen, and it's no one's fault, necessarily. By now, I'd sooner live with my memories than have fresh experiences that in the end will only turn to pain anyway. I didn't choose this life, it turned out like this because of my nature and various chance meetings and events. Perhaps different relationships would have made a difference, another job, children.

Sometimes I ask myself why everything came out this way, when it was determined how I would live, but there's no point in asking such questions. It's possible that the decisive factors weren't things that happened but other things that didn't happen. And all the rest can be taken care of by time, which went on its way, and made big things out of little ones, and turned chance into inevitability. The life I live is only one of many possible lives, just as this world is only one of many possible worlds.

I don't have any vivid memories of childhood. There's no reason for me to suppose it wasn't happy, but when I think about my emotional horizon at the time, I wasn't so much concerned with happiness and unhappiness as calm and disquiet, security and unsettlement, feeling protected and lonely. The clearest in hindsight is an almost constant feeling of astonishment at the phenomena of the world and the laws that govern them. Not only would I often lose my way, but I often couldn't find my way out of my own thoughts, and I spent a lot of time seeking for order or trying to produce it in any way I could. I drew up all kinds of lists, favorite books and favorite films, favorite food, friends and enemies, questions and arguments, just to gain some perspective on the world that confused me, that I couldn't understand. But my efforts produced little in the way of clarity; the more sophisticated my systems grew, the more I saw that they didn't really have much to do with reality, and gradually my astonishment at the world turned into a fear of its unpredictability.

———

A childhood memory. Christmas Eve. On the way to school, I have to walk past a field that in summer was planted with maize. It's early and still dark, and it's cold. The ground is frozen, and I walk right across the field, stumbling over the furrows and stubble. Halos have formed in the foggy air around the streetlamps beyond the field, and the orange orbs of sodium lamps light me the way. In the middle of the field, I come upon a half-burned-down white candle; maybe a child that, like me, was taking a shortcut across the field threw it away or lost it after the candlelit procession a few days ago. I press the candle into the hard ground and light it. What am I doing with matches? I stand there and watch the burning candle, a strange ritual whose purpose I don't understand and that yet seems portentous to me, it is an almost religious feeling.

If I believed in anything in the course of my life, then it was that there's a reason for everything, even if we can only rarely see it, and that everything we do has significance, even if we can't guess the consequences.

I will be late for school, and I won't have an excuse. My teacher will accept it, he knows there's no point in harassing me. I stand there and watch as the candle burns down and gutters out.

———

I can't remember ever being carried anywhere, I probably wouldn't have wanted to be. From when I was a toddler, I wanted to stand on my own two feet, and be left alone. Presumably, I never really cared for human society, I expected nothing from it, and soon understood that the way they would most likely leave me be was if I came up to their expectations and did what they expected. And you could ask me for anything—only not excessive proximity. Even if I liked someone, a teacher, a fellow pupil, a relative, or a friend of my parents, I did so more in thought, and was careful not to give myself away, and possibly awaken feelings I might not have been able to cope with. It didn't seem to bother anyone, I wonder if anyone even noticed. I was my only confidant, and I negotiated with myself as with a stranger in a continual silent dialog. Not only did I talk to myself, but I played out whole scenes to myself without realizing it. In my imagination, I could be anything I wanted to be, could master every task, prevail in every argument, win every girl. If the world didn't accord with my wishes, then I changed the imaginary version of myself, and came to live more in that fantasy world than in reality.

Seen from outside, I was functioning, I didn't create any great problems, was a good student, punctual and respectful and easy to deal with. Only on rare occasions, I would lose control in a sudden access of rage or indignation or self-pity, and shouted and rampaged and was impossible to calm down: I couldn't recognize myself. I went wild, like an engine that has nothing to hold it back. But, all things considered, I probably wasn't any more odd than other children, because we're all odd, if you think about it for long enough.

Another memory. How old was I then? A chilly Sunday morning, I wake early and get up straightaway. The house is quiet. It's snowing outside, the wind is blowing the snowflakes this way and that, like a curtain in front of an open window.

I'm outdoors, walking down the street. The snow muffles all sounds. But for the thin wisps of smoke rising from the chimneys, you'd think you might be in a post-human world.

A fire in the woods. The black charred wood in the white of the snow, the yellow and blue flames, the embers. Damp crawls into my shoes, my feet are ice-cold. Snow slips off a bough, the quality of the silence changes, the released bough bounces up as in relief, in slow motion, snow crystals trickle to the ground. The cold claims me, it's as though my body doesn't belong to me anymore, I could touch it like an object, my arms and legs, my trunk, my head, my hair. I run home, but something is holding me back, I move, but don't seem to make any headway.

To get a little order into my life, I set up rules for myself. To this day, I don't step on cracked paving stones, or if I do, then I do it with each foot equally. If I happen to fail, I feel an almost physical unwellness.

I did a lot of counting, my steps, fence posts, cars, men and women I passed on my way to school, total number of letters in words and sentences, regardless of meaning. I kept the figures in my head, some I grew fond of, and would repeat like a mantra, others I disliked, heaven knows why.

I liked ordering things, packing them up, I liked all kinds of containers, files, desk drawers, little plastic or metal containers, glass screw-top jars. For a while I made boxes of all sizes and lined them with marbled paper or cloth. Some I gave away, the others are still around somewhere.

I liked regularity and reacted angrily if my habits were disturbed. I was capable of spending long periods over meaningless tasks. Taking things apart and reassembling them calmed me. Or even just taking them apart, and ordering the parts, picking apart pieces of cloth or string into fibers, tweaking the needles off pine twigs one by one, or unpetalling a flower. I enjoyed drawing, but a lot of my drawings consisted of minutely penciled cross-hatchings that took me hours and hours, strange-looking landscapes, chains of hills, woods and meadows, cloud formations. Sometimes I would sketch 3-D views of complex geometrical forms on graph paper, works of pure industry, which after completing I would lay in folders and never look at again. Only rarely would I draw from nature, and then only small subjects, a flower, a leaf, a twig, my hand.

Will you give me one of your drawings? Franziska asked, having watched me during class. Maybe that hilly landscape? Where is it? There isn't a dwelling or a street on it, not a single person, only wooded hills and a cloudy sky. I had to stick two pieces of paper together to get that much distance.

I don't know what I did with the folder, maybe it's in the attic? It's bound to be somewhere. I'm sure I didn't throw it away. It's that you don't want to give it to me, isn't it, says Franziska. I have no idea why. There's nothing I value about the drawings, I never look at them, but they're like a part of me. If I gave one away, it would be like shrinking, diminishing myself, tearing off a part of myself. Franziska shrugs and walks off.

I was alone a lot, but I only suffered from loneliness when I was in the company of others. Ideally, I played by myself, or with fantasy playmates who did what I told them and came and went whenever I said. I think even as a child, I preferred staying home. And home could be anywhere where I was alone.

My *house*—it still doesn't feel natural to call it that. For me, it's my mother's house, even though she's long gone, and she deeded it to me. When I moved back into it, I didn't change a thing, and even later I only did the minimum of what had to be done, had some broken roof tiles replaced, the old boiler, the broken washing machine. The plumber wanted to dispose of the old one for me, but I asked him to leave it. Now it's standing in the garage, rusting away.

I like the house's gradual dilapidation, the peeling paint on the shutters, the crumbling putty in the windows. I like the spiders' webs in the corners, the dust on the books, which are for the most part those of my parents. I like the smell of the old bindings, the whole undefinable smell of the house, as it gradually evolves over the passing seasons. The smells of the seasons—another file that needs to be started.

Sometimes I sit in the kitchen or on the hallway floor where I often played when I was little, or on the bed in my room, and wait perfectly still for the memories to come, distant voices, bleached pictures, an intimation of feelings so remote that they no longer cause pain. The long, evenly passing years, all those breakfasts, lunches, and suppers during which there was never very much talking, and nothing that mattered. Sheer repetition, the knowledge that we would be sitting here tomorrow in the identical configuration, and the day after and next week and next year. Time seemed to be so abundant back then, it was as though there was no time.

I haven't changed anything in the garden either. I mow the lawn, prune the roses, and the shrubbery when it gets too overgrown. I make jam out of the blackcurrants and the raspberries, just like my mother. The mason jars pile up in the larder, I make more than I can possibly use. I pick the apples on the old apple tree, and store them until they're all old and wrinkled, and fit only for compost. There was a time I kept a couple of vegetable beds, but eventually that got to be too much work for me, and I neglected them, now they're covered with weeds.

I stand in the garden, adjust the garden furniture, pick a few weeds sprouting in the cracks in the terracing, and watch the birds. I walk through the house, sit down on a chair, get up again. I look at the old photographs on the sideboard, my parents, my grandparents, myself as a baby, as a small boy, I have no pictures of my own to add to them.

I walk into my parents' bedroom, where no one but my parents has ever slept. The beds are still made, as though they might return sometime. Perhaps it sounds mad, but I'm not mad. I just don't want anything to change, and what's wrong with that. To oppose the passing of time, not to permit oneself to be washed away with the flood of change. It's as though I lived in my memories as in this house, in a kind of continual present, where nothing disappears, only very gradually bleaches, dusts over, disintegrates.

I still sleep in my boyhood room, where I haven't changed anything either. On the walls are posters I put up when I was little, animal pictures in the main, a poster from an open-air festival I didn't attend, and an old type case full of junk, little treasures, colored glass figurines, a rifle bullet, souvenirs from holidays abroad, coins, decals, a shark's tooth, a music box that plays "La Vie en Rose," relics of an uneventful life, and yet every one of them capable of telling a story.

I sometimes lie up here to read, then I have the feeling my mother could call me or come knocking for me at any moment to wish me a good night and remind me not to stay up too late. The rain drums on the dormer window.

I have never slept with a woman here, maybe because it would have been embarrassing still to be in my nursery room, maybe because I didn't want to desecrate the place, disturb my memories. Has Franziska ever been here? Did she visit me when we were in middle school together? In high school? I no longer know.

But of course I did, she says, and on more than one occasion. Have you forgotten? I can't see you here. Did you sit at the desk, or stand beside the window? What did we do? We sat on the floor and looked at books of photographs. It was when you still wanted to be a photographer. Don't you remember? You showed me your camera and your lenses, the pictures you'd taken, experiments in black and white, blurs, macro-images, little still lifes of drawing pins and needles and pencil lead, you even took one of your toothbrush. She laughs. Did I ever take a picture of you? There were a couple, you let me have them, but I don't know if I've still got them or not.

There is Franziska sitting cross-legged on the floor, leafing through a volume of Ansel Adams, leaning right down over it to examine the tiniest details of the landscape. Her back is bent, her T-shirt has come untucked from her jeans, I can see a bit of her bare back and the elastic of her underwear. My camera is on the table, but I don't dare reach for it and push the release. You must have a look at this one, I say, turning to the bookshelf for another volume. I have a few paperback monographs of the famous photographers, Boubat, Werner Bischof, Cartier-Bresson, Brassaï, Man Ray, and next to those some alphabetically ordered little Reclam editions of texts we'd read at school, and a few textbooks from college. But it wasn't till much later that I bought those, the complete set of the Fischer World History series that I gradually acquired secondhand. I take down the first volume, *Prehistory*, edited by Marie-Henriette Alimen and Marie-Joseph Steve. I blow the dust off the top, turn a few pages, settle down to read the preface. The period covered takes in the millennia from the first dawn of mankind to the Iron Age. The prehistoric map is incomplete. Great tracts of time and space are left blank. Hominids of the early Stone Age, *Homo erectus*, Neanderthal and pre-sapiens.

I love those volumes in which the centuries, the millennia, the histories of peoples and continents are encompassed in a few hundred pages, even if I've never read them. Their mere possession is enough for me, the feeling that I have the entire history of the species in fifteen inches on my bookshelf. When I put the book back and turn around, Franziska has gone.

My *college years* were difficult for me. I had left home and was living in an efficiency apartment in a hospital personnel wing. It was all pine furniture, narrow bed, shelf, a school desk with two drawers, which I soon replaced with something bigger, a vast old desk that someone had wanted to get rid of. A friend gave me a small fridge that had gone through I don't know how many sets of owners and had been painted dark blue by one of them. On top of that I set an electric kettle and a hot plate, so as not to have to use the communal kitchens where all kinds of people were hanging around, preparing some very strange dishes.

From my window I had a view of part of the city, but much of the rest was obscured by the main hospital building, a discouraging-looking multistory lump with numberless windows at which people were busy being born, suffering, and dying. Sometimes a light would go on in one of them in the middle of the night and I wondered what that signified, if a patient had rung for a nurse in his agony, if there was a sudden emergency, someone was dying, or just couldn't sleep and was frightened of the dark. In spite of the drama that was surely taking place in the wards, the sight had something comforting for me, the thought that the patients were being looked after, that they were in good hands, that everything possible was being done for them, whether it happened to be enough or not. In all my life I've not been in a hospital, but since that time I've had no more fear of them, it appears to me like a last refuge, a place where I can give up all responsibilities.

Many of the inhabitants of the accommodation wing were shift workers, and for long periods I sometimes wouldn't see a soul. I hardly knew anyone at college either, and for the first time in my life I suffered from loneliness. It wasn't the exchange with others that I was missing, but the feeling of being connected, of belonging. All around me people were flirting and laughing and debating, but for some reason, which to this day I am unable to say, I was unable to join in their little games. Perhaps I felt ashamed, but then I wouldn't know what of, perhaps my mere existence was enough.

I felt best during lectures or in the great reading room in the library, among people and yet alone, engrossed in listening or reading or writing a paper.

This was the period in which historiography turned its back on great men and became interested in little people instead, in ordinary life, one's immediate setting, local history. We read Ginzburg, Borst, and Ariès, and were packed off by one professor with tape recorders into old people's homes, guest worker settlements, farmhouses. I hated these field trips, the chance nature of the assembled materials, and the mere thought of the quantity of what slipped through our fingers. I much preferred to work in the silence of the library among books and documents. This was before the time of computer terminals, everything was in card catalogs, these were worlds of paper, where time stood still, worlds that were very slowly growing, as though in a long inhalation. When the library closed at night, I sometimes had the feeling of having been put out like a dog, sent back into a world full of danger and uncertainty, and I ran back to the accommodation wing through the gathering dark, and crept into my room.

I remember a seminar on American history, where we discussed the Declaration of Independence. We hold these truths to be self-evident, that all men

are created equal, that they are endowed, by their
Creator, with certain unalienable Rights, that among
these are Life, Liberty, and the pursuit of Happiness.
I remember our professor giving us a long harangue
to the effect that Jefferson's idea of happiness
had nothing to do with personal fulfillment, and
everything to do with material possessions, that in
his concept every family should own and cultivate its
piece of land, a society of self-sufficient settler types.
I pictured them all on their rectangular plots, each
as white as a piece of blank paper, which they were
cultivating by the sweat of their brows and inscribing
with their narratives. It sounded like a hidden
imperative, to settle down, start a family, identify
and pursue certain objectives, and succeed in these,
a sequence that frankly terrified me. Presumably that
was when I decided to deny myself to all such things
and live my life as unbothered and unobserved as I
might.

My minor was philosophy, and for a time I even
thought of switching subjects to something where
field studies were not yet all the rage. I'd read an
article somewhere on an extremely rare condition
called congenital analgesia, or the innate inability
to feel pain, and I thought of writing a dissertation
on theories of pain and painlessness. I spent a lot of
time in the library, read and annotated all kinds of

philosophical, psychological, and even medical tomes. I had the vague feeling this analgesia was something to do with me, even if only loosely, as a metaphor. But I never succeeded in shaping my material in any way, and in the end I gave up. All I remember is that I had a theory of pain as the profoundest form of consciousness. A creature whose consciousness held only pain, I concluded, would have to live in a world consisting only of itself. We were able to feel ourselves through pain, we existed only because we felt pain, pain was our entire existence.

Even when I was a student, I rarely met up with friends, hardly ever went to the cinema or the theater. And each time I did, and went back to my room afterwards, I thought: why did I even bother.

During the vacations I found temporary jobs, I worked in offices or on building sites, and once I worked in the press archive, where I made such a good impression that I was offered a permanent job upon graduation, and where I ended up staying until I was let go.

Even when I was far and away the most senior person there, it never occurred to me to apply for a post in management. That was the only criticism leveled at me by my boss in our annual meetings: my lack of ambition. And that even though he moaned about the stream of meetings he had to attend, and his superiors who were putting pressure on him, and their decisions which he had to put into effect, even though he thought they were misguided, and couldn't understand why they had been made.

I liked life in the agency, the taut atmosphere in the editorial rooms, the telex machines spitting out the news in the form of endless ribbons of paper, the journalists who came and went, always in a hurry, always wound up about something. What I liked best of all was the late shift, as the editorial deadline approached, and the tension got even higher. Then, if there was some big event on top of that, an election, a revelation, a scandal, even back in the archives we got a little euphoric, felt fevered, had the sense that we were feeling the pulse of history. But I also liked the quiet mornings and the weekend shifts, when all you could hear in the section was the turning of newspaper pages and the clack of scissors as we cut out the articles that concerned us. Even today I still have the smell of paste in my nostrils with which we stuck down articles—that is, until we went over to using archive-quality Scotch tape instead.

I never quite understood what you found so fascinating about that place, says Franziska. I had asked her to lunch once, and then taken her back and showed her around, even introduced her to my co-workers, as though she was about to start working there. You told your boss I was a singer, and that you should start a file on me. He just smiled at that. That was shortly before the launch of your first CD, isn't that right? Or was it just after? It wasn't like that at all. I had come to the press agency to do an interview, my first ever, and that was how we came to meet. It was strange to run into you, you hadn't been in touch for ages and ages, and you were almost dismissive to me then, as though I had no business in your little world. I was just confused to see you in the doorway, and the editor calling out to me, look who's here.

The file was duly started, and each time one of my colleagues added an article about Franziska, they would let me know. That's your old school friend, isn't it, the singer? She came to visit us that time. Are you still in touch? Then people quit and new people came in, and my relationship with Franziska was forgotten.

In our pomp, we employed a score of people at the archive, but when computers came in, they were all gradually let go, photo archives and text were amalgamated, that too was something our boss had to break to us, along with the decision of who was going and who could stay. I couldn't have done such a thing. I was happy to always have the same work, to read, select, make order.

The traffic outside the house has almost stopped entirely, I hardly even see pedestrians go by when I sit at the window watching the birds at the feeder. I could have stopped feeding them long ago, but I'm going to keep at it until early summer, I like watching them, and I like their company, especially now, when the world seems to have fallen into a deep sleep. When the rain stops, I make up a list of things I need, and pick up my backpack a little earlier than usual.

I'm the only customer in the grocery store. The owner makes a few pithy observations about the state of the world. I want to give him what I owe, but he shakes his head and points to a dish next to the till. I wonder what that's about, but I don't say anything, put my bills in the dish and take out the change and put it in my pocket. While I stow my shopping into my backpack, the grocer disappears among his aisles without a word to me.

There's no one outside. Maybe that's the reason why, after months of inertia, I suddenly feel the impulse to go for a walk. So instead of going home, I head down the hill, in the opposite direction. There's barely any traffic on the main road, and when I get to the river and follow the path that leads up into the valley, I'm all alone.

Four sharpened sticks are propped against a tree trunk by the firepit. Presumably someone used them for grilling sausages and left them for some subsequent picnicker. Down by the water's edge I find the remnants of a small world put together from little twigs and fir cones; blades of grass and a few withered flowers are lying there, a pattern of pebbles that must have had some significance for the kid who made all this and left it behind. When it next rains, it'll all be washed away.

I sit down on the riverbank, the scene blurs, and I close my eyes. Images come up in the roaring of the water. Franziska and me at the baths, at the riverside, sometimes at one of the little nearby lakes. We cycled out there. It was a rainy day, but that didn't deter us, we both loved water and couldn't resist it. The little bathing place was closed, so we changed behind the hut with the changing rooms, back to back but so close that I thought I could feel Franziska's movements and the warmth from her body. We ran down to the bank, and leapt into the water, which was warmer than the air. We swam a long way out, rapidly and without speaking, as though we had some objective. A couple of ducks flopped across the lake, or they may have been grebes. Other than that, not a living being.

The water was dark, almost black, close in to the shore I felt the long tendrils of water plants that grew up to the surface and slithered along my legs. With each stroke, I dipped my head in the water. I kept my eyes open and saw Franziska's body ahead of me in the murk, a bright intimation.

She dives down, and I follow her into the dark. Now the water is suddenly clear, and in the remaining light I can see her slender form, the calm, powerful strokes with which she descends. She turns, as though waiting for me. Smiling, she beckons me closer. Her hair is floating around her head, it looks like the tendrils of the water plants. I am now very close to her. She takes my hand, pulls me in, and we kiss. Air bubbles up out of our opened mouths, from our bathing suits, I seem to hear the echo of a laugh. I try to grab hold of Franziska, but her body slips from my grasp. Then she takes my hand and pulls me farther down into the dark and the cold, and the deep which opens out. Suddenly breathless, I open my eyes. On the opposite bank, there is a man walking his dog.

There was one occasion when Franziska and I actually did kiss, on the corner where our ways parted each day. It was after the ninth-year end-of-year party. I had determined I would finally tell Franziska I loved her, even though it was something I could hardly explain to myself. We stood on the corner, it was past midnight, we were both tired probably, and didn't know what there was still to talk about, and yet we didn't want to go home either. After a long silence, I said the words I had said a thousand times to her in imagination: I love you. May I kiss you? I spoke so softly and indistinctly that she didn't hear me. What did you say? Only then, when I stolidly repeated my piece, did I feel how hollow and inadequate it sounded. It was as though all the wonderful and mysterious things I felt for Franziska had been reduced to those stupid words that were forever being spoken and worn away by others. There followed a short silence, then Franziska said: All right, you can kiss me, but I'm not in love with you. And the happiness of kissing her went under in the unhappiness of not being loved by her, and of secretly knowing that I didn't deserve to be loved by her and never would.

Even now, forty years later, I can distinctly remember that moment, the words we spoke, the corner where it all happened. I remember Franziska, her smile and her brief hesitation and even her kiss, which in spite of its brevity was more than friendly, only myself I don't remember. In the images of the past, in the place where there ought to be me, there is a fog, an absence. It's as though the boy I was occupies the space of my memories but never existed as a living person.

I still remember how huge and disturbing my love of Franziska was, but the sensations associated with it get weaker and weaker, until I'm afraid one day all that will be left of it will be a kind of rote insistence, like those formulaic expressions in old letters that leave you so unconvinced when you read them.

There is another sentence, and I don't know if Franziska said it or my memory invented it. I don't love you because I love you. How do you mean? I ask. You said it, says Franziska, and laughs.

Two ducks swim upriver and cross the rapids with a few quick wingbeats. The noise of birds in flight, there's something else I need to start a file on.

Under the old-fashioned hat rack next to the front door, there's a large cardboard box full of empty manila files that I buy from the same wholesaler where the press agency bought its files. I take out a couple and mark them up, The Sounds of Water and The Sounds of Birds in Flight, then lay them on top of a pile of at least a dozen or more other such titled but still empty files on my desk. I don't know what I'm going to fill them with, I've always collected and sorted and ordered things that others have experienced and written down.

I go down to the basement to my files, leaf through the thesaurus that contains the whole world broken up into subject headings and classifications and subgroupings, a sophisticated number system. Arts and Entertainment. Music. Principles, Forms, Ensembles, Voices, Instruments. Musical Traditions. Vocal Music. Lay Music. Songs of Western Light Music. Biographies. Here is the file for Franziska, or Fabienne, as she called herself later. Originally, there used to be a separate alphabetical index of persons, but I gradually broke that down and incorporated it, and found for each person the correct place in the system, for politicians, artists, sportsmen and -women, it took weeks of work and many difficult decisions.

I take out Franziska's file, weighing it in my hand. It must be about four pounds, I need both hands to hold it, that's how hefty it is. I take it up to my office, put it on my desk, and for a long time just look at it.

Fabienne is the title it's been given. Sometime, when the archive had already gone over into my possession, I wrote *Franziska* underneath, and put her date of birth in parentheses alongside it: 19 May 1965. I left room on the right for a further date.

Days go by. How long has the world been standing still? Time seems to make no odds. I go walking more, almost every day now. I go along the empty streets and gradually get used to being out again. If I pass someone, which doesn't happen often, I give them a wide berth, change direction, sometimes even turn back. I don't have anywhere particular to get to, after all, and it hardly matters if I go this way or that. Already at the end of a week, I can't imagine how I stuck it out for so long in the house, but I notice too that my moods are more volatile than was previously the case, sometimes I'm over-happy, almost delirious, then, when I'm outside, I get a burst of fear, my breath stops, and I feel dizzy. Then I need to grab hold of something, a lamppost or tree or a fence post, till I've calmed down, and can make it home. There I hunker down in the basement for hours until I'm fully recovered. Suddenly I have a fit of rage, I hate the archive, which seems like a dungeon to me where I've locked myself up. At one point, I'm close to ripping the files off their shelving and trampling them underfoot, but what good would that do?

That night, I dream of it all burning down to the ground, my whole archive, the house, all my things, and it isn't a nightmare. No one comes to quench the flames. I stand in front of my burning house, dangerously near, and yet I can't feel the heat of the fire or smell the smoke that climbs thickly into the sky. All I smell is the lilac, which this year has bloomed rather earlier than usual.

I open Franziska's file, a thick pile of articles, interviews, reviews, even some pieces she wrote herself. It must be thirty years since her first public concerts, a girl with a beautiful voice and great expectations.

This may sound a little strange, but I hardly ever read the files, I'm just happy for them to exist and be kept up to date. I've not even ever looked up Franziska's file, just as you don't look at the days you've spent with someone you love. You live them one after the other, and each new one takes the place of the one before, settles on top of it, a further layer in the sediment of memory. When I open the file, I have the feeling I'm committing an indiscretion, as though I'm doing something I'm not allowed to.

I don't know what I'm looking for. My slowly fading memories of Franziska? But maybe it's not my images of her that are fading, perhaps it's me becoming ever more translucent, losing my vigor, till eventually the only reason I'm alive will be because I lack the strength to make an end.

The newest articles all concern Franziska's breast cancer. She had made a point of not letting on all the time she was ill, had carried on as before with an enormous effort of strength and willpower, bought a wig and given concerts and interviews on all sorts of subjects, everything but her cancer. Only when she had survived the disease did she talk about it with the openness and bravery that one looks to from celebrities. But even in those conversations which were all about her health, her body, her fears, she seemed strangely absent, as though her illness was just another kind of public appearance, to be negotiated with her customary professionalism. I ask myself, was it down to her or the journalists, was the public even interested in what might be concealed behind the façade of that made-up face and frozen smile. And was there even anything there?

This all happened four years ago, and then things grew quiet around Franziska, as though her overcoming the illness had only sealed its victory. No new album, no concert tours, no new partner, not even one of those articles where journalists wonder aloud what has become of this or that celebrity, when things have been quiet around them for some time. After all the years in which I'd collected every little scrap I could find about Franziska, this withdrawal of hers struck me as something of a betrayal.

I remember all the partners the popular press were pleased to accompany from beginnings to break-up, the mysterious first boyfriend whom she wouldn't even name to the journalists, and who quickly left the scene anyway, to be replaced by the next one, the producer who had discovered her and was responsible for her early recordings. Next there was the soccer star, and then the singer she sang the duet with and then bedded, and all the other men who were the subject of remorseless speculation. Who is the man with Fabienne? Has she got a new fellow? Is it true love this time or just a flirt? I turn the pages, read the headlines, A proper night's sleep is like a holiday for me, Success is so unbelievably stressful, Love came through his text messages, The loneliness of the long-distance singer, I've got nothing to lose.

Each time one of Franziska's relationships came to an end, she would claim she was all through with love, she was perfectly content without a man, could look after herself, she was quite happy as a single.

Those were always happy, hope-filled months for me, till the next time she turned up with a man at her side. What was I expecting? That she would give me a call after ten, twenty, thirty years, and tell me she'd made a mistake, she had loved me after all and still did, I was the love of her life as she was the love of mine? Of course not. I think it was enough for me to know that she, like me, was alone.

I look at the oldest articles, A cup of coffee with . . . a brief interview with Fabienne, who will be presenting her first CD in the Volkshaus tonight. *I Am Who I Am*. Odd title. I wonder if it's a conscious play on Holy Scripture, and if either of us, she or I, was aware of it at the time. I crank up my old PC, and quickly track it down, Exodus 3:14, Moses asks God what his name is, and God replies, I am that I am. Tell thy people, I am hath sent me unto you.

The translation at this point seems to be uncertain, the search lists all kinds of variants and commentaries. In one of them, I read that the correct translation should read, I will be there who will always be there. And in another: I am the one who is present. An oddly modest appellation for God, nothing like Almighty Creator, the Master of the Universe, the Stern Patriarch, only the one who is there, the one who is present. The designation would just as well fit me, certainly as regards my relationship with Franziska, I was always there, not as a protagonist, just as a distant observer and escort. And yet, it was my secret hope that Franziska would feel my being there, my thinking of her, that it might make for an invisible connection between us, even if we hadn't seen each other in decades. She turned up in my thoughts, talked to me, commented on my doings, gave me company, supported me, joked with me. Then we would look at one another silently, and hug and kiss and make love. Of course, that was all nonsense, but the idea that I was with her as she was with me was a comfort to me.

I pull out a manila folder and write on it: The One Who Is Present, and put it on top of the pile of other empty folders.

The first interview was pretty banal, with Franziska jokily trying to duck out of the journalist's boorish questions. Something she would never do, not even for lots of cash? Something that was sacred to her? Whom would she like to spend a night with? Where did she like to be touched?

Was she currently in a relationship? the man asked, and she replied, yes, but she wouldn't say any more than that. That must still be the enigmatic first boyfriend who is alluded to in a couple of other

articles as well, but no one seems to have seen him
or known anything more about him than that he
existed. I wonder who it might have been. She and I
were spending so much time together in those days
and talking about everything under the sun, I feel
a bit miffed that she never told me about him. But
maybe she just wanted to spare my feelings because
she guessed I was still very much in love with her.
Franziska had always been discreet in personal
matters, she had never gone along with home stories
or aired her dirty linen in public, but at least with
her other partners you knew their names and there
were photographs of joint public appearances.
Occasionally she would talk about personal things
too, how she was going to be spending Christmas
or where she was going for her holidays. I look at a
couple of the later interviews, but soon get bored.
Franziska had this noncommittal way about her, she
would give the reporters what they wanted and yet
still not say anything significant or revealing. Every
single hour I spent with her, I felt I had learned more
about her than from this whole stack of paper.

It's gotten to be suppertime, but I'm not hungry
and don't feel like making anything. Nor do I
switch on the evening news, more and more I have
the feeling I've heard everything before, and that
I'm turning round and round like a Möbius strip,

without any chance of escaping. Sometimes the
sun shines, sometimes it's cloudy, sometimes cold,
sometimes warm, there's nothing I can do about it.
I open a bottle of wine, pull on a warm coat, and sit
out in the garden behind the house. The sky is clear,
it hasn't rained for weeks, the moon is almost full.
It's rare for it to be so close to the earth, it said in the
newspaper, and it really does look bigger than usual,
almost alarmingly so. For days I've felt a disquiet,
as though I'm being threatened by something or
someone.

Franziska and I never talked afterwards about
our kiss, nor about my love for her either. But our
relationship seemed to change after it, it may even
have become more intimate. I was grateful to be close
to her, and she seemed to like having me around. We
walked to school together and spent a lot of our free
time together too. I knew that Franziska liked singing
and sang beautifully, and that she took lessons in it,
but she didn't talk to me about her ambitions.

   After completing school, she took a course in
nursing at the local hospital, and I went away to
college. We saw less of each other, we probably both
had our hands full of adjusting to our new respective
environments and making our way. Or could it be

the student finds he has more interesting society in the university, says Franziska. So many pretty girls from good backgrounds. It's easy to forget about a little nurse then. That's not true, I say furiously, I have not forgotten you. But you haven't been taking any trouble for me, she says.

Most likely, we saw each other in the holidays, when we were both visiting our families, and inevitably felt stifled at home, and arranged to meet in the old bar. We drank beer, played pinball, and talked. The bar was smoky and loud. And once we saw in the new year together, do you remember, says Franziska. We cooked together in the block where you were living. There was me and a couple of the other nursing students and that friend of yours, what was his name again? Walter? At midnight we went up on the roof and we could see right across the whole city and the lake and the fireworks that people were setting off. I'd forgotten all about it, but just now it came to mind again. It was a freezing night, and I was completely crazy about you. You stayed the night with a friend, and I took you there. Later that night I walked back to the accommodation block, all sobered up from the cold and feeling happy.

When we met up, I never talked much about my life at college, and Franziska barely mentioned nursing and the hospital, instead we went over old memories, our old teachers and classmates, really as though we were more interested in their lives than our own. I was surprised when Franziska told me she would be singing some songs at their graduation party and asked me to come along.

Before she came on, we were together backstage, she was terribly nervous, it was as though she was about to appear on television in front of an audience of millions, and I tried to get her to relax. I spat over her shoulder three times, and she said, you're my lucky mascot. Then she sang some songs by Barbara, difficult, melancholy things that didn't seem to me to suit her at all, and that moved me all the more. I stood in the wings and watched Franziska from the side. She seemed more beautiful than I'd ever seen her, really grown-up for the first time and strong and yet vulnerable. She sang about love and pain, fulfillment and loss, as though she'd experienced all of them, and it was as though that gloomy anticipation made her more beautiful than any amount of pain.

The applause was halting, and at the buffet later on I heard a couple of Franziska's colleagues doing down her performance. The songs hadn't been appropriate, all that mournful stuff, this wasn't a funeral, and another person said Franziska seemed to think she was a big star, well, she'd have done better applying herself to her exams. I suppose I should have stood up for her, but I didn't, just pushed off rather sheepishly. I don't know if those aspersions reached Franziska at all, she seemed strangely absent all that evening, and more earnest than usual. When the music and dancing began after the snacks and speeches, she told me she wanted to go now, and would I walk her home.

My studies seemed to go on and on, without my being able to say why. I frittered away my time, achieving and undertaking little. Franziska had taken a job at the university clinic, and we saw a bit more of each other. We went to films and concerts together, stayed up half the night talking, but never about relationships, it was as though neither of us was quite ready for that.

That said, Franziska seemed much more grown-up than I did. She was living in a little studio apartment, and had bought a secondhand car, a 2CV, which she took for some hair-raising drives. From time to time, she had concert engagements in little places in the country. I would drive her, help her setting up, sometimes man the very basic sound system or take entrance money, and late at night, when she was still all euphoric after her performance, drive her home.

If some member of the audience got a little persistent, I would step in and keep people off, while Franziska disappeared backstage. If the concerts were too far to drive, we would stop overnight in a rudimentary hotel or B and B; sometimes, in the interests of economy, we would even share a bed, like brother and sister.

The concert organizer had come with the key, because the inn closed at ten. This was somewhere in Southern Germany, the Black Forest maybe. Even though he had given us a detailed description of the route, it took us a long time to find the place in the middle of the forest. It was an inn with a large, slightly run-down beer garden, and a couple of rooms over the bar. The night entrance was around the back of the building. We couldn't find the light switch and felt our way up the stairs. Franziska took my hand and led the way; I thought of Hansel and Gretel, lost in the woods. No, says Franziska, we're *Brüderlein und Schwesterlein*. The little brother is changed into a deer, and each time the horns sound for the chase, he wants to go into the forest. He wants to go hunting, even though he's the quarry. And then he gets hurt, and still he won't change, the next day he wants to go hunting again. Isn't it awful—both beautiful and terrible at the same time? You were always afraid of the hunt, though, weren't you? she says. So I'm the little brother, and you're the little sister. And she laughs her laugh which makes me feel giddy.

The room was old and pretty run-down, there was just one big bed, a half-collapsed sofa that looked as though it had come out of a dumpster, a wardrobe with a mirror. The heating barely worked, it felt cold and damp, and there was a weird smell. Franziska took it all well, it felt pretty miserable, but she was laughing and joking the whole time. We whispered to each other, though we were pretty sure we were the only guests, and probably the only people in the whole building. Maybe there are wolves? she said and looked at me with big eyes, I think she must have been a bit tipsy. Why the big eyes? I asked. The better to see you with. And why do you have such a big mouth? she asked and winked at me.

There was an opened bottle of wine from the concert, and in the bathroom we found two plastic cups in cellophane wrappers. I poured, and we drank. To your success, I said, long may it continue. Too bad you don't play piano, said Franziska, because then you could be my accompanist and we could go on tour together. She emptied her cup at a single draft, and said she was going to wash. Shortly after, I heard the whooshing of the shower. It seemed to take forever till she emerged from the shower, just in underwear and T-shirt. I was still sitting on the sofa, and she stretched out beside me, laying her head in my lap. I'm so tired, she said, and smiled, seen perpendicularly and from above her face looked completely different, she seemed younger, more open—open to what, I don't know. I brushed the hair out of her face and stroked it. I ran my finger along the side of her ear. She wasn't wearing a bra, the nipples showed through the thin T-shirt material. What are you looking at? she said and laughed. In my recollection, I then stroked her breasts very gently, her belly, but is that even possible, or am I just making it up, because I wanted to so much. No one spoke. Eventually, Franziska sat up and said she felt cold and was going to bed. Will you come?

I went into the bathroom and washed and cleaned my teeth. Then I just stood there for a long time, staring at myself in the mirror, I have no idea what I was waiting for. I held my breath and listened for sounds from next door. When I finally went back into the room, Franziska was asleep. I lay down beside her. Without waking up, she moved closer, and pressed herself against me.

I've often thought about that night in the forest inn, imagined how things might have been different if I'd come out of the bathroom a little sooner. Perhaps Franziska had been waiting for me to make the first move. She had said she didn't love me, but that was years ago, when we were still children, and feelings can change. After driving her home the next day, I wrote her a letter, but reading it back to myself it seemed so tangled and indecisive that I threw it away. Or did I keep it somewhere? I can't remember. All I know is that I was never as much in love in the rest of my life as I was then, always simultaneously happy and despairing.

Sometimes when I saw her, I could hardly breathe, and once or twice I burst out crying after she was gone. It seems a little bit mad to me now, crying over a woman, but I'm not sure if that's maturity or indifference. The last time I cried was after my mother died.

What would I write Franziska today? I've always loved you? I've waited all my life for you? No, I didn't wait, but I was always there. I was always there for you, even if we never saw each other. Perhaps it's as well that we didn't get together, a relationship wouldn't have been enough for my love, it could only have damaged it, worn it away like an object or an overused word. Why did I happen to fall in love with you? I can't say. I can as little explain it to you now as almost forty years ago, when you told me you didn't love me. In all those years, I haven't gotten any wiser, just older.

I've opened a second bottle, after all, what difference does it make? It's dark in the garden, the streetlamps are all blocked off by the house. I can hear something rustling, maybe a hedgehog. Are hedgehogs active so early in the year? I'm not sure. Do I have a file on hedgehogs? I'm not sure either. How many things there are that I don't know the answer to.

Later, in bed, this crazy idea comes to me. That first, unidentified boyfriend of Franziska's was me. The longer I think about it, the more certain I am. I'm sure she would have told me if there'd been someone else, one of our friends would have let me know, I would surely have noticed something. He would have accompanied her to her concerts, but I was the only one doing that. Or perhaps, by claiming she had a boyfriend, she was merely protecting herself from the lunatics who fell in love with her face or her voice. Men were always writing to me, says Franziska, I kept getting these weird letters from people who behaved as though they knew me. Some wrote me their sexual fantasies, others proposed to me, or told me their net worth, one sent me a picture of his house and car. Letters like that used to frighten me, even if they were mostly completely harmless.

I suppose I was just another one of those madmen
who declared their love to Franziska without really
knowing her. How many letters did I write to her,
without mailing any? Have I still got them? Have
I got a folder on love, or my love? Where would I
file it? Under Sociology and Anthropology, Social
Interactions? Or maybe Medicine and Health,
Illnesses, Psychic Abnormalities?

The peonies are sprouting. The rootstock must be
fifty or sixty years old, maybe more, they were already
there when I was a boy. I water them, they're robust,
but this year really is exceptionally dry. Have I got a
file on peonies? It always bothered me that gardens
and flowers were always q.v. Agriculture, and not
under some artistic heading like Landscape Art or at
least under Natural History, like the other plants. I've
of course considered a reorganization, but that would
be to interfere with the system. I can't wantonly
interfere with the system, just because some element
of the thesaurus doesn't meet with my approval. It
can be limitlessly extended, but it can't be changed.

I should have been back at my desk long ago,
but of late I haven't really felt the inclination.
Unprocessed newspapers and magazines are piled up
on the floor, it will be weeks before I've worked my

way through them all, but even that thought fails to motivate me.

I can't remember what made me apply for the year abroad, it may be that I thought if I was in Paris I wouldn't be any more unhappy than I was at home. Or was I actually trying to get away from Franziska? Did I think I could give my emotions the slip that way? Who's going to drive me to my concerts? she said, when I told her. Then she laughed, and it almost sounded as though she was relieved. She congratulated me on my scholarship. I always knew you were going far, she said. Will you come and see me in Paris? I asked. Sure, she said, if you set me up with a concert at the Olympia. But she didn't come. The whole year I was gone, I heard very little from her. She sent me the occasional bland little postcard, the weather was great, she was doing fine, she hoped I was too. Then, on one card from her summer vacation in Italy, she suddenly wrote "we" for "I." We're loving the Italian cooking, going on lots of outings, we've gone a deep brown. I wondered about that "we," had she gone on holiday with her parents, or a girlfriend, or a man. I set the card down on the little desk in my room, and would sometimes spin it around and read it again, as though I could catch

Franziska out, and so discover who she had gone on holiday with.

If the point of Paris for me was to get free of Franziska, then I was at least partially successful. My love for her didn't get any less, but I did sometimes wonder if I wasn't in love with love, and might I not feel as much for another woman. Then another postcard would come from her, she was doing fine, how was I, Paris must be amazing, she had never been. I read it a hundred times, looking for hidden messages. Did Franziska want to visit? Was she waiting for me to invite her? I had invited her. Was she missing me? For a whole week I could think of nothing else.

I was living in a cheap pension near the Gare de l'Est, it was a suggestion from a fellow student who'd stayed there awhile. My room was on the fifth floor, there was no elevator, and I had to share a bathroom with fifteen or twenty other long-stay residents, a lot of students among them, most of them foreigners like me, but also some folks who were in regular employment and couldn't find or couldn't afford a place of their own.

We were a curious bunch, that often went out together. It was the first time I'd felt easy in a group. Maybe it was the anonymity of the city that felt liberating. We each had our own story to tell, but it rarely came up. We could be whoever we wanted to be, we could experiment with a different kind of life. Almost every evening some of us would meet up in the bar next to the hotel for a drink. The fellow running it was an Algerian who went by Paco, and sold cassettes and dodgy leather jackets out of a back room. But none of that bothered us, on the contrary, it confirmed our sense that this was life. Everything was possible, everything was allowed.

We lived cheaply, ate in canteens or inexpensive restaurants, went to the cinema together, and lectures and concerts, or just prowled through the city talking. Shortly before my arrival there had been student unrest, with one kid actually getting clubbed to death by the police, I think it was about student fees or restrictions on admissions, I don't remember. In the end, the government had given way, and the air was still charged with the euphoria of the protests and the triumphant outcome. The students here were much more vocal than we were back home, we debated about books and films, conducted political and philosophical arguments, as though it was about to be our turn to rule the world. For me the whole thing was all a big game, I knew I was going back to Switzerland afterwards, and all this stuff was none of my beeswax. But all the more enthusiastically I waded in. I unwound, and at the same time the

toughness of the city made me grow up. I learned
how to get my way, I walked tall, and when I spoke to
people I looked them in the eye.

The pension is where I got to know the girl with the
dark hair. She was Swiss like me, attended language
classes and lived on the fifth floor. We adopted her
in our gang, and she would sometimes eat with us or
accompany us on our prowls through the city, even
though our conversation didn't seem to interest her
much. Most of the time she just sat there in the role
of the silent mysterious woman, and we showed off in
front of her. In fact she was more mature than the lot
of us with our wild theories and views and plans.

I didn't do much college work. I signed up for a
couple of seminars and heard the relevant lectures,
wrote the papers and comprehensions they asked for.
The seminars were held in a poorly lit underground
room in an annex, that early in the morning smelled
of bleach and cafeteria food. More than once I
practically fell asleep because I'd only gotten to bed
in the early hours, still hungover from the night
before. The actual student life happened after the
lectures in the local cafés where we met up to make
plans for the weekend or the evening ahead.

One Sunday in early autumn, one of those
warm sunny days where only the blackness of the
shadows lets you know that it's about to turn dark
and cold, we visited the Père Lachaise Cemetery.
I think there were six of us, me and my three best
pals and two women, the girl with the dark hair and
a hysterical Italian I didn't like and whose name I
can't remember. Chattering away, we walked around
the immense site, I wanted to see the grave of
Oscar Wilde, and take a picture of Edith Piaf's for
Franziska, and my friends were after Jim Morrison.

I was talking to the dark-haired girl and noticed
that the others had left us way behind, and that
there was just us two. Will you take a picture of
me? she asked. I had almost a full roll of film in my
camera and took a picture of her. Wait, she said, ran
her hand through her curly mop, and kept striking
different poses, different expressions, the shy girl, the
surprised-looking young lady, the seductive femme
fatale, clumsily imitated clichés that had something
rather pathetic about them. Then she took a couple
of shots of me. So that I remember you, she said,
forgetting it was my camera. So that I remember
myself, I said. When I got the pictures back later

from the developer's I almost didn't recognize the girl, and so perhaps saw her as she was.

That's enough now, I said, taking the camera out of her hand. Aren't you cold? she asked. I shook my head. Are you? A little bit, she said, and I took off my jacket and draped it over her shoulders. Our friends were gone. The girl took my hand, and we went on in silence now, a couple.

Eventually, we must have caught up to the others, because I remember trying to pull my hand away when they came in sight. But the girl kept hold of my hand and didn't let go until we all walked into a café near the cemetery. It was a big empty place with covered billiard tables in it. I wonder why I should remember that, even though it's so completely unimportant? The others didn't say anything, it was as though they had decided long ago that we two belonged together. Only now did I remember that I had forgotten to take a photo of Edith Piaf's grave.

Back at the hotel, the dark-haired girl came back to my room, as though it was a foregone conclusion, and I was again happy that no one said anything. I didn't feel anything for her, but her unfamiliar and unanticipated proximity got my heart racing. I can still picture the scene, it's dim in the room, we haven't turned the light on, the girl's lying on the bed, she hasn't even taken off my jacket, and is waiting for me to lie down next to her. I can't remember kissing, or whether we took our clothes off, how long we stayed in the room, whether we went out for a meal with the others. All I know is that a couple of days later I was in a pharmacy buying condoms, and the old pharmacist gave me a look as he handed over the little package as though it contained medicine against an awful illness. I can't remember the first time I slept with the girl.

On my jaunts through the outer suburbs, the town seems unfamiliar to me, I am discovering it all over again, the way I discovered Paris then on my long walks. Everything looks different, beautiful, new. It's like watching a film that's all distance shots. If I see a human being, it's in the distance. We seem to repel each other like magnets with identical polarities. That's how I imagine the lives of early hominids, negotiating the wilderness alone, hunting, gathering nuts and berries, and if they happen to meet someone else from the species, they steer clear of them, after all there's enough space and food. Then eventually warriors make their appearance, they have realized that it's simpler to steal food than to collect it. They don't avoid others, they make straight for them, and kill them or subjugate them.

Larger groups are formed, which ambush others, steal their provisions, take their wives, butcher their children. Their genes are passed on, they are not fitter than the others, just unscrupulous. And the feeble and the timorous attach themselves to them, put themselves under their protection, and participate in their horrors, just so that they're not alone, so that they as well can have a sense of being among the victors. The odd loner persists here and there. They hide in caves, in huts, block off the entrances, only emerge at dusk when there's no one around. They do not want to be among the victors, don't want to join with any others, they just want to be left in peace. As if.

A young woman is sitting on a bench in a little park, telephoning. She has a loud voice, but I can't understand a word. She seems agitated, it sounds as though she's sobbing, then suddenly I'm not sure if she's crying or laughing.

The family of my girlfriend in Paris owns a hotel in Basel, a reputable place with a restaurant famed for its cuisine. My girlfriend was going to study at the hotel school, it was all arranged that she would enter the family business and eventually take over the running of the hotel. This was why she had been sent to Paris to improve her French. A lot of the hotel staff came from France, and a number of the guests as well. You could take a cooking course, she said, then you could manage the restaurant, and I would run the hotel. I don't think my gifts lie in that direction, I said. But we were young and didn't really think about the future and the kind of lives we would have after our time in Paris was over.

Do you love me? she once asked me, out of the blue. I can't remember what I said, just that my reply disappointed her. Everything's always so complicated with you, she said. Do you love me then? I asked, and she said yes so promptly, she might as well have said no.

Was she like me then, your Paris girlfriend? asked Franziska. No, I said, she didn't look anything like you. She was very pale, her skin was practically translucent, and she had freckles all over her face. She had curly dark hair and heavy eyebrows. There must be pictures somewhere. Do you want to see her?

I get out a file folder and write down the name of the dark-haired girl. Then I go up into the attic and manage to find the box with all my old photos in it and take it down to my office.

The photographs and the negatives are all together in the envelopes in which they came back from the developer's. I hadn't looked at them since, pictures of school occasions and family trips, my first trip on my own (to London), bad black-and-white pictures, an inventory of sights, Tower Bridge, St. Paul's, Oxford Circus, Hyde Park. I'm not in any of them.

The envelope with pictures from Paris is right down at the bottom of the box. They look exactly the way I remembered that first walk in the cemetery. Oddly, most of the ones I took of the dark-haired girl are slightly out of focus. And in not one of the shots she took of me am I looking into the camera, at her. Then there are a few pictures of graves, among them one of Edith Piaf's—and I was so sure I hadn't taken one. If not even that's right, then what's left of my memories? In a court of law, the picture of the grave could be used against me—luckily, no one's taking me to court here. I wonder if I ever made a print of it for Franziska. Presumably not. What would she think if I sent her one today?

I wonder if I've still got the letters my Paris girlfriend wrote to me when I was back in Switzerland. I've spent my life sorting and arranging, but in my own papers, and my life, there is no order, it's just an assortment of experiences, encounters, decisions that followed one another more or less randomly, and left their traces. There may be a pattern here or there, but that's an illusion, just like the shapes one can make out in the clouds, and which say more about our fear of formlessness than about the condition of the world. Maybe I'm afraid that not much would come out if I ever started to make an inventory.

I am sitting at my desk, a huge old chunk of oak that I bought cheaply when I was a student from a firm that was introducing contemporary office furniture. At the side it has a little metal plaque with the logo of the company, and an inventory number. I've never thought to have the plaque removed, possibly because I liked the idea that even my desk was inventoried somewhere as part of a greater system of organization.

I've moved several times with this desk, but I never bothered to empty the drawers, and just shoved them back in with their contents when I got to the new address. There must be things in there that I stashed away twenty or thirty years ago, without much thought, and never took out to examine, fossils of my youth. When I die a company of movers will come in, maybe look around quickly for money and valuables, and then bundle everything up and take it to a junkyard or garbage disposal. Then, apart from a few kilojoules of energy for the urban heating, nothing will be left of my life. Presumably the files will also be disposed of, I mean, who's going to be interested in those. Amazingly, the prospect leaves me cold. Maybe it would even be right for the archive to leave when I do, it's my world and my life, and just as it one day began so it will one day end. When you build something up, you mustn't think about it all disappearing again.

I dig around in the drawers without finding anything of interest, a batch of postcards, a rubber stamp, matchboxes from various countries, old bank statements, instructions for appliances that aren't around anymore, notebooks in which only the first page or two have any writing in them. Even my grandfather's watch isn't an heirloom but a cheap mass-produced item. I turn up a couple of diaries for years long past. The entries include appointments with hairdressers and doctors, visits to the cinema, there are a few names, most of which don't tell me anything, or vague memories at best. They were maybe colleagues, university chums, chance encounters. A week in the Engadin, a fortnight in the South of France, this was after I broke up with my Paris girlfriend, I was away by myself on my motorbike, but after a few days I got bored of ticking off the sights, and spent most of my time sitting in cafés or up in some hotel room, with a book.

It wasn't long before my Paris girlfriend moved out of the hotel. She found herself a small apartment, unlike the rest of us she had money and standards. Her place was a couple of hundred yards from the hotel, but the distance couldn't have been greater. I continued to lead a rather primitive existence with my friends, eating and drinking, roaming through the city and talking about our plans and dreams, as though there was no such thing as the present that in any way concerned the rest of our lives. When I was with my girlfriend, everything felt much more concrete. She had a story in which I played a part, even though it wasn't clear to me what the part was, whether I wanted to play it, whether I could even play it. We played the life of the young couple with prospects. I brought her flowers, she cooked for me, there were candles. She vanished into the bathroom and came back in her nightie. Before we made love, I went and brushed my teeth. In the mornings, I got croissants not from the bakery down the street, but at a different one a couple of streets away, where my girlfriend thought they were better. I had never previously bothered my head about there being such things as superior and inferior bakeries, but she thought such things, and they mattered to her.

Her apartment was furnished, but even so I kept buying her things for it, a nicer cover for the bed, a vase for flowers, a frame for the Kandinsky poster she'd bought at the Pompidou Center. She gave me a diamond-patterned pullover that I never wore. Why did all my girlfriends always give me pullovers, all my life? Were they worried I might die of cold?

I never gave you a pullover, says Franziska. You weren't my girlfriend either. Did I in fact ever give you anything? I wasn't looking to you for anything, I didn't want possessions anyway. I thought at the time that things were only a burden on you. Now I've got a whole house full of junk and paper and I still don't feel secure.

My Paris girlfriend was constantly giving me something or other, a heart-shaped eraser, a tiny notebook in which I never wrote a word. She had a well-ordered bourgeois life and tried to integrate me into it. But I wasn't always welcome to her. We would meet up twice a week, three times at the most, for these strange performances of adulthood, on the other days either she had no time or didn't feel like seeing me, and that was fine by me. Our life as a couple felt pretty constricting as it was, and not quite right, even though I wouldn't have been able to say what was wrong about it. Maybe—and this would be the simplest explanation—maybe I simply wasn't old enough or sufficiently in love for a regular relationship.

The winter semester went on into February. I started taking my studies a little more seriously now, maybe I was just bored with the constant pub crawls, or it was something to do with the season, anyway, I was spending more time up in my room, preparing for the semester exams. Then they came, and a week later I was standing in front of the glass-fronted boxes where they posted the results, going through the endless lists to see if I could find my name. At that moment I knew that something was over, even though I hadn't really noticed it, and that left me feeling both liberated and melancholy. For a few days then I didn't see anyone, just walked around the city, with the sense that I was seeing it properly for the first time.

I could have stayed on in Paris with my girlfriend until my courses resumed in Switzerland, but for some reason I didn't do that. Her language course had another two or three months to run, and then she was returning as well. I can't remember the reason, but I remember writing her a note that I pushed under her door one morning, and that she turned up that evening in the hotel in tears, and that

we made up. It was a drama then, and just the shade
of a memory today. The day of my departure came.
She took me to the station, it was early morning,
cold and rainy, as it often was that winter. I think
she enjoyed the emotional parting. She had once
again come with a present for me, I have no idea
what it was, and she kissed me for a long time on
the platform, it probably looked like a scene from a
movie. When the train pulled out, she waved until I
could no longer see her. That was the last time I was
in Paris.

I sometimes tried to imagine what my girlfriend
will have done after my departure; maybe she bought
a croissant in the good bakery, made herself coffee,
and went back to bed, then she called a girlfriend and
arranged to meet in a café or one of the department
stores she was so fond of. To be honest, I had no idea
what kind of life she had when I wasn't around, but
when I thought about her life without me, I had the
feeling there wasn't much missing from it.

The letters are probably still somewhere that
she wrote me, I'm sure I wouldn't have thrown
them away. And lo, after hunting around for a
little while, I find them in a shoebox labeled Old
Letters, a collection of cards and envelopes and

Christmas cards that I kept for unknown reasons, postcards from people whose role in my life I've entirely forgotten, letters my mother wrote me in Paris, a single letter from my father. There's a bundle of letters stuffed inside an envelope with the name of my Paris girlfriend on it. I take them out, and recognize the handwriting right away, a plump schoolgirl scrawl.

Some of them she must have written to me while I was still in Paris, the envelopes are unstamped and just have my name on them, the rest she wrote after I returned to Switzerland, endless series of things she did and people she met. At the end of each one, she assured me how much she was devoted to me, and how much she missed me. In one scrawl on a stray sheet of paper, there's something about an argument, and she asks whether I was attacking her deliberately, and why was I so cruel, she didn't understand it.

Then there are some other pages, none of them dated, where she's writing about nice times, and how she's missing me, even though we can only have seen each other two days before. I remember one long back-and-forth between us, but all that seems as trite now as these letters. Things that happened to me, people I met, none of it has anything to do with me, none of it explains who I was at the time and who I've now become.

————

However wretched the relationship was with my Paris girlfriend, I still suffered from our final break a few months after she returned to Switzerland. We met up in Basel once or twice, she even introduced me to her parents, which was a peculiar gesture, given that our separation was clearly imminent. Her mother was nice to me, but her father let me know that he didn't think much of me and my relationship with his daughter. At the end of the summer vacation, my girlfriend was starting hotel school in Lausanne, which meant we were still more distant from one another. The letters grew less frequent, the kisses and assurances more formulaic. Among the letters she wrote me is one I wrote to her and never posted, which presumably was just as well. It wouldn't have provided much in the way of clarification. When I read it now, I start to wonder a little about my memories; I'm not quite sure now whether it wasn't her leaving me, not me leaving her. I remember stopping off in Lausanne on my way to the South of France. We had been going to go there together, but she canceled at short notice, she had exams right afterwards, and needed to prepare. I remember her sitting behind me on the bike, and how we took the metro and ate at a restaurant down by the lake, but I can't remember where I spent the night, whether I was with her in her room or in a hotel by myself. Did we have a falling-out, or make love one last time? I can see myself swimming in the lake, but I don't think she was with me. The lake scared me with its extent and the great dark depths I could feel below me. I stay close in to the shore, swim back and forth parallel to it, later on I'm lying on a meadow in some kind of park. Maybe I went on the same day?

The last letter from my girlfriend came months later. It started just as blandly as the earlier ones with all the things she'd been doing, and complaints about how difficult the classes were. Then there were suddenly all these passionate pleas to me to leave her alone. There was no point in me continuing to write to her, she wrote, if I didn't know what I wanted. Have a good life, she ended. I never heard from her again.

It takes me most of Sunday and Monday to get the letters in the shoebox into some kind of order, but at the end I'm still left with a number that don't form part of any correspondence, letters from people who only wrote once or twice, or postcards with illegible signatures, wedding and birth announcements that

I only kept out of piety or indifference, also the odd death notice. Letters from male and female friends that formed part of an extended correspondence I file away, in chronological order, in individual folders named for their senders, though that's a superficial form of organization, and not really satisfying. In some ways, the unsorted confusion before was the more appropriate order.

I have also filed away Franziska's letters in a separate folder, but there aren't many. Early on, we saw each other so regularly there was no need to write, then once she became successful, we lost touch. Only in between there was a brief period in which we exchanged letters regularly. I was back at college, finishing up my degree, Franziska had transferred to a clinic in Graubünden for training as a psychiatric nurse. I like the letters from that period, because for the first time she was writing about her feelings and asking me for help and advice. She felt out of sorts in the mountains, the landscape depressed her, and so did the plight of her psychiatric patients. She wasn't getting along with the rest of the intake, she wrote, and was feeling lonely. She still had the occasional gig in some school or club, but there was nothing that suggested that she would ever be able to live from it. Come visit, and we can go hiking, or to the hot baths.

I was still suffering from the separation with my Paris girlfriend, I'm not sure if I told Franziska about it, but I suspect I didn't. Presumably I didn't tell her anything about that relationship, the whole thing felt like a betrayal of her, even though she had no claim on me.

That may be the reason why I kept postponing my visit, looking for excuses, approaching exams, term papers I needed to finish, anything. When I finally went up in the early summer, she'd been there for over a year.

I don't remember much from the day I spent with Franziska. I see us walking up a deep gorge, with a waterfall at the top end of it. A picnic lunch on a meadow beside a clump of firs. The sunlight is very bright, the shadows practically black. I can remember a tartan rug, wood ants suddenly all over everything. The water in the stream is ice-cold, in between places where it is fast-running there are deep crystal-clear pools. Did we bathe in one of these, or is that another fantasy of mine? Did we even have our swimming things with us? I seem to see Franziska in a bikini in the shade on the tartan rug, with her eyes closed. I am sitting beside her, putting out my hand to touch her, then taking it back. Her eyes open,

and she looks at me. We speak, but I can't hear what
we're saying, our words are drowned in the roar of
the stream, which dominates the entire day, a bright,
living, roar that never stops and never gets quieter.
I look at Franziska, try to interpret her expression,
her smiles, her movements. Am I your girlhood lover,
whose name you refuse to tell anyone? Do you still
love me? May I kiss you again? Are you waiting for me
to kiss you?

You never asked me any of that, says Franziska.
You told me about your year abroad in Paris, your
studies, your plans for the future. I was so lonely
up in the mountains, and I had been really looking
forward to this day, but I had the sense there was no
room for me in your life and your plans. And then
you just left me.

We take the post bus, get off at the train station
in Chur, it's dark already. The last train that would
take me back to the city leaves in a few minutes.
You can always stay with me, says Franziska. Did
she really say that? But I have a seminar tomorrow
morning at eight. Aren't you conscientious, she says
and smiles sardonically. Not conscientious, I say,
so much as there's only seven of us and my absence
would be noticed. I've yet to miss a class. I don't
know why I'm talking so much rot, the whole time
I'm thinking how I can fiddle things so that I can stay

overnight without giving Franziska the impression I wanted more. And while I'm still stuck for words, she says, well, safe home, and she turns and goes. The train conductor whistles and calls all aboard, and I run to the train and ride through the evening down to the Unterland.

I've never noticed before how many church bells I can hear from my garden, maybe their ringing is swallowed by other sounds the rest of the time, the constant hum of cars on the highway, the street noise, factories, and building sites, which is almost muted. The bells ring for noon. Didn't we sing a song in kindergarten about the twelve o'clock bell? Here goes the twelve o'clock bell, time for me to go home as well. Or almost time? The midday demons is a notion I picked up somewhere, I can't remember where, but it made instant sense. It's not night, it's noon that's the preferred time of demons. Then it's as though the sun is stuck at the zenith, and briefly all kinds of things are possible. Even the birds seem a bit freaked out, they are hushed, and only come out of their hiding places when it's afternoon.

There still hasn't been any rain, the earth is dry, there are brown splotches on the lawn, and little cracks in the soil. I ought to water it really, but at this hour I can't get myself to do anything, not even go indoors and eat something. I am sitting in the shade of the old apple tree, perfectly still, as though the demons would get hold of me if I betrayed myself by the least movement.

I visited Franziska once more in the mountains. There was early snow, and she had said she wanted to go skiing. I was happy when the weather on the appointed day was so dreadful that I thought I could leave my ski equipment at home. But there was Franziska waiting for me at the station in all her gear. We could still have gone, she said, disappointedly, the lifts would have been practically deserted, we would have had the entire slope to ourselves. We decided to take her gear back to the accommodation block where she had a small studio apartment. You can carry my skis back, she said, given that I lugged them all the way here.

It was far too warm in her room. The furnishings were cool and plain, a bed, a little desk with a matching chair, an armchair in the window, a little cooking niche. Franziska peeled off her ski suit, underneath she had on some beige thermal underwear. Sexy, don't you think? she said. I'll put some other clothes on. Or do you want to stay here?

In the end, we spent the whole day in Franziska's room, talking, drinking tea, listening to music. Franziska sat on the bed, I sat in the armchair, we both sat on the bed, then we both lay there, she on her back, I on my side. Franziska sat on the chair backwards, with her arms across the back, I stood by the window. She went up to me, still in her thermals, just with the sleeves pushed back. Her cheeks were flushed with the warmth. I ran my hand down her back. Your fur is as soft as a bunny rabbit's. They want me to sing in German, she said, and maybe even write my own words. They say they can really imagine me going places, but not with those French songs, which are apparently really out of fashion. Can you write words?

Who do you mean: they? I asked. A producer I met at a workshop. He says I need to call myself something else too. How about Fabienne, I said, without much thought, that's a good name for a singer. She laughed and said, but it's meant to sound not French! I can't play the piano, I said, I can't write song lyrics, and I didn't bring my skis. I'm no good for anything, am I? You're my friend, she said, and stroked my back, the way I had stroked hers a moment earlier. Promise me we'll stay friends, whatever happens.

It wasn't until much later that I asked myself what she had meant by that. Whatever happens. I was waiting for you to kiss me, says Franziska, but I was afraid to lose you as a friend. You would have slept with me, and then you would have left me to do whatever you had to do. And you would have felt so bad about it that your conscience would have prevented you from getting in touch again. You wanted to go abroad again, get a doctorate, you didn't have any space for a steady relationship. That's not true, I said. You know that's not true. Then why didn't you kiss me?

Will you sing something for me? I asked. What would you like to hear? The song you sang at the graduation do. She seemed to understand right away what song I meant. She turned away from me and began to sing in a quiet voice. *Dis, quand reviendras-tu?* Her voice grew louder and more confident, and for the first time I understand how much her movements were part of the music, and that the music emerged from her movements and was made from them. In the middle of the song, Franziska broke off, turned to face me again, and smiled bashfully. It feels funny to sing that for you, she said.

She stood by the window, and started drumming on the sill, and then singing an unfamiliar song to me, "Liberté." It ended with the cry, *Liberté! Liberté! Liberté!*

Couldn't you translate some of Barbara's lyrics into German? I suggested. You could do that much better than me, she said, your French is so much better. Freedom! Freedom! Freedom! I said, that's easy. The other one is harder. Tell me, when will you come back? that's the meaning, but it gets tricky with the rhythm. Do you at least know that all the time that passes can hardly be captured, that all the lost time can't be captured?

Franziska leaned on the windowsill and looked me in the eye and didn't speak. I crossed to the sink and ran myself a glass of water.

I found the lyrics on the Internet. I'm not sure if it was just generally embarrassing for Franziska to sing for me, or if it was those particular words that made her feel awkward. What does it matter that I still love you, what does it matter that I always love you, what does it matter that I love no one but you, when you don't understand that you have to come back? I make of us both my loveliest memories, then I go on. The world delights me, I will warm myself at a different sun, I am not one of those who will die of grief. I don't have the virtue of the sailor's wife.

But who listens to song lyrics anyway? If there was the amount of loving and leaving that goes on in songs, then the world would be a different sort of place. The thing that exercises me is something else.

All my life, I was convinced that Franziska didn't love me, that I was nothing more than a good friend to her, maybe even for a time her best friend, and for that reason never a potential lover. Now all at once, I see all the signals she sent me, possibilities she created, invitations to come to her, to tell her my love, to kiss her and love her. Was I too blind to notice at the time, or was it my shyness, or did I secretly not want to get together with her?

You see, now you admit it. I don't admit anything, I'm just wondering if that's what happened. How our lives might have changed if I'd kissed you at the waterfall, if I'd embraced you in your room, if I hadn't taken the last train. Imagine I'd gotten pregnant that night, says Franziska. She laughs, but I don't think it's funny.

I remember a conversation with a colleague at work many years ago. He and his boyfriend had just split up, and he said he had had enough of love, he would have been happier in his life if he had never been the object of someone's grand passion. Or did he say victim? I can remember how incensed I was at that. My colleague was surprised at me, of all people, taking up the cause of a great love. But you're coming at it from theory, not practice, aren't you? he asked. I was so mad, I stalked out of the little kitchenette. What did he know.

But maybe he was right. Maybe I was too afraid of losing Franziska for me to seriously try winning her. Whereas my unhappy love, my dreams, my fantasies, no one could take those from me, not even her.

I have finally abandoned my plan of integrating the newspapers and magazines of the past few weeks. I know it's a sacrilege. A hole will be made in the archive, which is something that has never happened since it's been in my possession. Even when I was off sick for a few days and bedridden, I caught up on everything I had fallen behind with. But this is too much, I can't possibly catch up, it's more than I can do to work up the newspapers that come in every day. Even taking them out of my mailbox sours my mood, touching the rough dry paper, smelling the acrid printer's ink. I have to wash my hands each time.

For days now, I've been toying with the idea of getting in touch with Franziska. I know who to call to get an address for her, an old colleague from editorial who often covered her and even claimed to be a friend of hers. I asked him to say hello to her for me once, but I doubt he ever did.

I don't know what made me think of it, but I've started making paper airplanes out of the publications, the way we used to do when we were little. All the current affairs articles take wing, important government legislation, commentaries from politicians and scientists, also sports reports, recipes, travel tips, personal columns, they all become airplanes, float off, and come to rest in some dusty corner of my office.

On the Internet I find instructions for folding origami figures, and I make fishes and birds, swans, cranes, and land animals too, horses and elephants, foxes and hares, I spend days folding until my fingers are stiff. At last the paper is becoming animated, my desk is full of them, and before long the dinner table and the bookshelves and the floor, an entire world full of tiny animals. I can hardly walk out of the room without crushing one of the tiny creatures underfoot.

After two months without rain, the weather has finally turned, it's cooler, there's a wind blowing, and it's started raining, first cautiously, then gradually more heavily. As though it had taken the wind to get me moving, I finally called my colleague. He's home. He tells me some tales of office life, a sacking, a love affair, some bickering. It doesn't interest me one bit, but I have to listen, after all I want something from him, and am dependent on his goodwill. When he finally stops and I'm able to get in my request, he gets all pompous. He had earned the confidence of the stars by not abusing their trust. But Franziska and I went to school together, I say, we're old friends. That's neither here nor there, he says, sometimes old friends are exactly the people they don't want to hear from.

He could be right about that. I don't even like myself in the role of someone who pops up out of the past simply because he's got it into his head that he wants to settle certain matters that should have been settled long ago. What's the point of these old stories? Have we really got any more to say to each other than it said on one of Franziska's old postcards: I'm doing well, how are you? The sun's out, and I'm busy. Though of course I'm far from busy.

In the end, my colleague gives me Franziska's email address, and makes me swear not to say it was him who gave it to me. And if you get wind of anything interesting, give me a call, he says, we've not heard anything from her in donkey's years. I promise and get off the line.

My colleague failed to ask me a single question, not even how I was feeling, or what I was up to. Presumably the memory of me has already started to fade in the agency, but then I never wanted anything else anyway. As far as my colleagues were concerned,

I was never anything but one of the gray mice who did the research, dependable helpers whose job one day was superseded.

I leafed through Franziska's file some more, this time looking at the pictures, but even with them in front of me, I'd have a hard job describing Franziska's appearance. I can see the color of her eyes and hair, I see the style, the mouth, nose, brow, but all that doesn't make her, that's not what I loved about her. I look in the box of old photographs again and find a couple from when we were young. Franziska's always in the middle, they are group snaps or shots from school trips or parties. In one of the pictures, she's holding a guitar and maybe singing. I'm there in the picture too, eyes down, bashful and spotty, with a worried-looking smile. I don't look at all comfortable in my skin, as the saying goes; presumably I couldn't begin to imagine what Franziska found attractive in me. At least she seems less strange to me in these photos than in the magazine shots. It looks as though she'd learned a couple of expressions for the press photographers and the audiences, none of which corresponds to her true being, or says anything about her. There's always the same stereotypical smile in the carefully made-up face that is for everyone.

I ask myself what it does to a person, always being on show like that, and having to put on some kind of expression so as not to be recognized. Maybe that's why I hesitated for such a long time to write to Franziska, for fear there was nothing left of her.

The last time I saw Franziska was at the presentation of her first CD at the Volkshaus. I had been sent an invitation, a printed card, which she had signed in thick felt-tip. We're happy to welcome you to the launch of the first CD by Fabienne, the latest star in the Swiss pop heaven. Another one of those undefined "we"s. There was nothing personal on my invite, no greeting, no please come if you can, not even her real name. I picture her sitting at a table in the office of some agent or producer, with a stack of cards in front of her, signing them mechanically, one after the other, without even looking to see who they were going to.

The foyer was full of people, the only ones I recognized being Franziska's parents, who were standing in a corner looking thoroughly out of place, and whom I avoided as well as I could. I felt pretty out of place too with my plastic beaker of prosecco. I was happy when we were told to file into the hall, so that the show could begin.

The producer thanked the audience for coming, and then gabbled a few words about Fabienne;

the first time he heard her voice, he said, he had
straightaway recognized the awesome potential
there. Then Franziska herself walked onto the stage,
wearing a short white dress with lace trim, and so
heavily made up, I hardly recognized her. Two thirds
of her set consisted of love songs, usually broken
relationships, but with a little hope still left. A day
without you. Are you still on your own? Let's try
again. You, only you! Missed you rhyming with kissed
you, sunshine with be mine, alone now with coming
home now. At the end of the concert, the producer
walked back onto the stage, put his arm around
Franziska's shoulder, and yelled a few words to the
audience that went under in the applause. Then
he gave her a kiss, and the two of them wandered
offstage. As the applause refused to stop, Franziska
came back out and announced that for an encore
she was going to sing a song by Barbara, an artiste
who had powerfully influenced her. Whereupon she
sang—unaccompanied—"Litanies Pour un Retour,"
a piece I had heard her sing earlier. After the poppy
tunes in the rest of her set, this seemed to go over the
heads of most of the audience, but the feeling was so
good that Franziska was forgiven.

I had hoped to catch a word with her, but she was
besieged by all kinds of people. When I finally caught
her and offered my congratulations on her debut, I

was just about to ask if she fancied having a drink with me sometime or going out somewhere when her producer turned up to drag her away and said he wanted to introduce her to the nation's leading music critic. The last look that Franziska threw my way was hard to parse, it looked half frightened, half resigned. For a moment I wondered if she'd been taking drugs, but then I dismissed the idea, it was probably only the excitement that made her pupils look so dilated. I've never taken drugs, says Franziska, I couldn't afford it. I wouldn't have managed if I had. A drink, sure, and sometimes one too many. As you could see for yourself when you used to drive me to concerts. I lift my coffee cup and toast her absent glass. To you, my invisible companion.

The producer's kiss, and the proprietorial way he put his arm around her, had aroused my suspicions. Soon after, I read in a magazine that they were going out together. Yes, he's my new friend, she told the interviewer, but that's all I'm going to say about him. My new friend.

The producer was fifteen years older than Franziska, and he looked another ten years older than that. I could not understand what she saw in him, or why she would love him. The idea of them sleeping together turned my stomach. But the man seemed to be a gifted promoter, in no time at all,

Fabienne was everywhere, you could read about her beautiful voice, her slim figure, her cheerful, girl-next-door nature. Pop Kitten, they called her, Golden Tonsils, later Pop Princess. In autumn I finished my degree. That's twenty-nine years ago now.

> *Dear Franziska,*
>
> *I don't know if you remember me. A long time ago, we were school friends, and maybe a little more than that. I've followed your career over the years; as an archivist, I was close to the source, and collected and ordered innumerable articles about you. Five years ago, I lost my job, but I kept the archive going as a personal project. In the last few days, I've been thinking about you a lot, I don't really know why...*

Of course she'll remember me, you don't forget the friends of your youth. But what will she think of me if I tell her all about my archive? She'll think I'm a loser, someone who's lost his job and can't get traction anywhere else. Or worse, that I'm a madman who's stalking her and collecting material about her. Maybe that's what I am. Suddenly my whole life looks pretty wretched to me, it's as though I hadn't ever really been alive, just watched others in their lives, and waited for something to happen. And nothing happened.

I delete what I've written and go out into the garden. The rain is still falling gently. In the dusk, there's a quiet ticking to be heard, as though the ground were soaking up the moisture, stretching out, breathing. Close to, the drips are falling in varying rhythms, forming ever new syncopated patterns. Then a motor wails, someone steps on the accelerator, I've heard that a couple of times these past weeks, it sounds like a fit of rage or a burst of wild joy and enthusiasm.

I must write to Franziska today, tomorrow I will no longer have the willpower. I don't know what makes me quite so certain, but I feel this is my last chance. But I can't push myself.

I sit in the garden, it's getting dark, the rain stops, starts again, very gently, and stops again. I imagine myself just sitting here, immobile, not eating or drinking again, not even waiting anymore. I will be as quiet as a plant, the rain will wet me, the sun will dry me, the sunbeams nourish me. Little shoots will emerge from my fingers, my toes will drill into the ground, form roots, I sit in my shadow, time passes.

It must be the church bells that have roused me. I look at my watch, it's a little past midnight. Even though it's not cold, I'm shivering, shuddering all over my body.

Dear Franziska,

it's been too long since we were last in touch. It would be nice to see you again and talk about old times.

Best wishes,

Without thinking about it anymore, I press send and go to bed.

Now that I'm no longer working in the archive and have stopped reading newspapers, the days seem endlessly long. My walks have gotten longer and longer, by now they are real hikes not just crisscrossing the city, but deep into the surrounding hills. What continually surprises me is how much of what I see looks unfamiliar to me, even though I've lived here most of my life. I always followed the same routes, not looking either left or right. I wonder how many streets there are in my town that I've never been down.

For a little while I select a neighborhood and systematically walk through all the streets like a messenger boy with deliveries for everyone, but I quickly get bored with that, resume my old aimless walks, and let fate guide my steps.

At home, I have to force myself to not keep checking my emails to see if Franziska has written back yet. I take a book down from the shelf that I meant to read for a long time, but I'm unable to concentrate and soon put it back. I listen to an old Barbara recording that Franziska once gave me for my birthday. I'd gotten to know some of the songs by heart, and when I was by myself belted them out at the top of my lungs, "Göttingen," "Dis, quand reviendras-tu," "La Solitude." When I sing along to them now, my voice sounds cracked, and I've forgotten half the words.

The grand emotions, the beseeching, the protestations of love, all those strike me as false now, maybe they always were. Tunes and lyrics were the work of others, and when I sang along to them, I wasn't sure if they were expressing my feelings or producing them, like germs penetrating the body and making it ill and feeble.

Ever since I can remember, I have doubted my feelings, and even in the greatest upsurge of emotion, I have had a tendency to stand to one side and observe myself. I can remember the way I threw tantrums as a child, and at the same time watched in fascination what effect my behavior had on those around me. Perhaps that's why I was so overcome by my feelings for Franziska, because they seemed to come from my body, not my brain. Because I didn't understand them and couldn't even properly name and classify them. That may be why I did all I could not to fall victim to them.

It rains all day. I open the glass door onto the garden, sit there and feel the cold air coming in and touching me. The rain whispers, and inside that whispering like little jewels are other clearly defined sounds like the squealing of bicycle brakes, the laughter of a child, the screak and chatter of birds.

The fact that Franziska's producer was so unworthy of her eventually seemed to comfort me in some strange way. To my way of seeing things, it was purely a working relationship. He lived in Germany, she lived in Switzerland, and they were both continually on the road. Almost more jealous than of her partner I was of the musicians with whom she appeared, the singers she sang duets with, or was photographed with. They gazed deeply into each other's eyes and swore eternal fidelity in song.

Then all of a sudden there was her new man, the soccer star. I wondered what the story was there, and what could have induced Franziska to turn away from her producer. The fact that—later on as well—

she was often leaving men was like a promise that she would do the same thing for me one day, once I had the courage to declare my love to her. Even if only in my imagination.

Franziska and the soccer player had met at some event or other, a gala or charity ball, I don't remember. I open her folder again and find an interview the two of them gave together. They had been a couple for a while at that stage and had just moved in together. Franziska said the soccer player had written her love letters after their first meeting. Was he such a poetic character, then, asked the journalist, and the soccer player said love had lent him wings. If that was the standard of his letters, I was frankly astonished that Franziska fell for him. She said he was exactly the man she had always been looking for, generous, honest, and open. The difference in their ages didn't bother her, no, no, quite the contrary. The journalist asked if she believed in love at first sight. No, she said, not in my case anyway. But I do, I say aloud, and the sudden sound of my own voice makes me jump. I fell in love with you instantly. Then why did you give up so readily? she asks. Why did you not just keep telling me that you love me? Why did you not conquer me?

But then do you believe in the grand passion that most of your songs are about? asked the journalist. I feel it, she said. Then they got onto babies, and you could tell from their replies what a difficult subject it was for them both. After all, they had just moved in together, they said, and they were both taken up by their respective professions. Plus the soccer player had two children from a previous marriage that he was part-responsible for—Franziska got on very well with them, she assured the questioner. The journalist wouldn't let go until Franziska said she would probably want to have children eventually, but she didn't want to rush anything. After all, she was still only in her early thirties.

Then she was forty, and fifty, and now she's fifty-five, same as me. She never had children, not with the soccer player with whom she was together for eight or nine years, not with her next friend, the singer, and least of all with me. Had she got involved with all the wrong men after all?

What about you, she asks, did you never want children? I don't know, I say. And I really don't. If you and I had gotten together, if you hadn't been a singer, then we would have had a wholly different life. When you were stepping out with the soccer player, I had a lover, a colleague at work. I made her pregnant, but she never told me, and she had an abortion. It wasn't for a long time afterwards that she told me about it. How did you react? I was surprised. And then I was amazed at how little it affected me.

We had gotten together at round about the same time as Franziska and her soccer star. Was there perhaps a connection? I was thirty, had been working in the archive for four or five years already, when a new colleague was hired. She was a little older than I was, a Germanist, who had previously taught at a university, but she had enough of academic life, the wrangling and the competitiveness. I was assigned to show her the ropes. It was summer, and the town seemed like a wilderness to me. The broiling air over the hot asphalt, the sky pale with heat, the noonday silence, the few people who dragged themselves along in the shade of the buildings like shy beasts, it all seemed to me the way I pictured the steppes, and it wouldn't have surprised me if, say, a herd of gazelles had come galloping along the road. First there was just a cloud of dust in the distance, then heads, legs, trunks, approaching. The noise grew louder, the energy of their motion filled the air. Then the herd pushed past, the drumming of their hooves hung in the air, and finally disappeared in the haze. The dust settled, and then everything was quiet again, and just as torpid as before.

The air in the archive was humid and hot, even though we kept the blinds down all day. Our boss had given us instruction to rearrange something or sort out something, the number and size of the folders was by now so huge that their administration and streamlining was enough to keep us busy around the clock, even with no research orders and fresh reports coming in.

For weeks my new colleague and I had been sitting facing one another at one of the big tables, sorting through mounds of paper. Sometimes, to explain something to her, I would go around and sit next to her. She was wearing a white sleeveless top, and her bare arm almost touched mine. I saw a small dark stain at her armpit and smelled her deodorant and a faint whiff of sweat. We just sat there, not speaking. There was electricity in the air as before a storm, we had no control over our bodies, they just seemed to be drawn to each other. My colleague got up very slowly, she seemed to be moving in slow motion, and walked over to the shelving, though she wasn't doing anything there. She leaned against a shelf and laughed, and said, Strange. We looked at each other, not saying anything. I can explain that to you later, I said, and returned to my place on the other side of the table.

After a few days we started to talk, and over time we talked more and worked less. My colleague had a keen sense of humor, and we laughed a lot. She had discovered that on the back of the articles there were often the most peculiar things: announcements from inventors looking for funding; graphologists, clairvoyants, and astrologers touting their gifts and offering their services; cinema and theater programs with long-forgotten films and plays. Weren't you born in 1965? she asked and proceeded to read me a death announcement from that year, the unlooked-for deaths, so it said, of a mother and her son Michael. It could have been you, she said, suddenly serious, imagine a son Michael, an unlived life. Then she started laughing again and read an advertisement from something called the Sama Vega Institute, offering help with blushing, inhibition, and panic.

What most tickled her were the personal ads. Here's one for you, she said suddenly, charming widow of sophisticated elegance, 49, lonely for the past two years, villa owner, seeks to meet with a view to marriage cultivated, faithful, and generous gentleman of distinguished mind, healthy optimistic outlook, and possible car. I don't know if I quite fit the bill, I said. What, the possible car or the optimism? Anyway, she's almost twenty years older than me. Well, to be exact, she's eighty-four, said my colleague, if she's even still extant. But what about this one? 31-year-old Catholic girl, tall, dark, slim, 5' 8", employed in medical profession, wltm mate for life, who appreciates sweet girl. Not a day under sixty-six now, I said. What makes you think I'm looking for a mate? Why, have you got one? she asked. Can you appreciate a sweet girl? Is there nothing there for you? Well, maybe this one, although he's forty, which makes him seventy-five now, but he's looking for an honest maiden of between eighteen and thirty. And he enjoys a good income and owns a sports car. I wonder what happened to all those people. Did they find the spouse or good Catholic lady of their dreams? I always find those ads a bit sad, I said, the way people toot their own horns, and what they seem to value in themselves and others. Well, I think they're funny, said my colleague, turning the page. Back to race riots in the USA.

As we both liked swimming after work, it seemed we might as well go together. Better just meet down by the lake, said my colleague, it wouldn't do to let the others think there was any funny business between us. She laughed and twinkled at me, even though you don't even own a sports car. I know a place that's usually pretty quiet, I said, and told her how to get there.

When we met on the little patch of grass after work, there were only a few people there, most of whom I'd seen there before, older, single people for the most part. A woman was there with her dog, which was leaping around like crazy in the water, barking and splashing. There were no changing rooms, so we got changed under our towels, and swam out for quite a long time. When we got back, the meadow was deserted, but for one woman with a book, and a pair of lovers who were getting tangled up without much inhibition. Is what they're doing even allowed? whispered my colleague and laughed. If it's for the survival of the species, I said, the answer is probably yes.

We lay side by side on our towels, and I could feel the same electricity in the air as there was a few days before in the archive, but this time we didn't seek to oppose it. My colleague turned onto her back and looked me in the eye until I started kissing her. That night, we slept together for the first time.

We spent a beautiful tempestuous summer. The fact that no one at the agency knew about us only heightened the tension and the pleasure. We kissed clandestinely between the shelves, sometimes we were close to having sex there. My girlfriend wore short skirts, I pushed them up, she undid my belt, and shoved her hand in my pants. She laughed breathlessly. We're out of our minds, she whispered, what if the boss catches us here. A door opened, and a voice called out: Hallo, is anyone there? It was one of the journalists who often came with extensive research requests. Just coming, I said. My shirt was untucked, and I quickly stuffed it back, and did up my belt. I grabbed hold of a folder and stepped out of the shelves. The journalist took a peek at my file. Creation Myths? Who are they for? It's an external request from a schoolboy, I said drily, but he seemed not to be listening, and just filled in his order. How long will it take you to find this for me?

In the meantime, my colleague had stepped out too, also with a folder in her hand. Her cheeks were flushed, and her hair was tousled, but the journalist was already on his way out. Here's the folder you were looking for, she said, still a little out of breath. She handed me the file, it was called Ideas of the Godhead, she must have grabbed it from the same subject area as me.

Following this incident, we exercised a little more caution, but it was only a matter of time before word got around the agency that we were an item. It was no big deal, relationships at work came about all the time, and the archive had a fairly obscure existence within the agency. As long as we did our work efficiently, no one was really interested in what else we got up to.

I was with my colleague for eight years. To this day I don't really know why we broke up, but I expect it was my fault, just as I was always to blame for the end of all my relationships. If I had to make a list of the faults my girlfriends found with me over the years, probably dithering would come first, followed by unwillingness to accept responsibility, absent-mindedness, and emotional coldness. Maybe that's why they all bought me pullovers.

In that case, we wouldn't have been such a bad match, says Franziska, my lovers all held similar things against me. Maybe both of us just aren't made for love? Or just long-distance love?

After we had broken up, my girlfriend told me she had aborted a baby of mine early on in our relationship. I don't know if it was her intention to hurt me by telling me. Neither of us had really wanted children, we barely spoke about it, but now she was making me responsible for the fact that she wouldn't have any, she had little time left, and had wasted it on me. I heard her out, even though her reproaches seemed unfair, and their endless repetition made me impatient. But I have never liked making scenes with people, and besides we were still colleagues, and it would have been unpleasant to have been on bad terms with her.

What world are you living in? said my girlfriend. Have you got any feelings at all? No normal man feels like that. I didn't say anything, what could I have said? I've watched you sleeping, she said another time, with a sad voice, though it sounded like a threat. The notion of being watched in my sleep, utterly defenseless and at her mercy, made me shudder.

I tried to deal with her as normally as possible, but that only seemed to drive her into deeper fury. Sometimes she would punch me in the shoulder when we passed each other, so hard that the bruises came up. But I didn't react to that either, I stuck it out, as I had stuck out all her nonsense in all those years. Finally, she handed in her notice, and however I regretted her losing her job on my account, I was also relieved not to be the victim of her moods anymore. Franziska's relationship with the soccer player ended about the same time, after he'd caught her cheating on him.

When I was walking around town today, something strange happened. The outer suburb I was walking through was, as usual, deserted. Suddenly, as I was passing a school, a boy of ten or so shot out from behind a corner and stopped and pressed himself, breathing hard, against the playground wall a few feet from where I was standing. I had stopped from surprise myself, and looked at the boy, but he seemed entirely concentrated on his pursuers, maybe they were playing a game of hide and seek, or else he was being chased because he had hurt someone or taken something. Far and wide, there was no one else to be seen, only this boy who struck me as resembling a frightened animal. Gradually his breath slowed, but he still wouldn't look at me. I had the sense he was living in a different world that I could maybe see into, but never exist inside. After some time, the boy slunk off, still in the lee of the wall, and then was gone, as suddenly as he had appeared.

Back home, I turn on the computer. Franziska still hasn't replied. It's three days since I've written to her. I'm tempted to write her again, but in the end I leave it. The worst thing would be if she got the impression I was stalking her.

Her folder's still open on my desk, to the interview she did with the soccer player. They are both smiling up at me, but they don't really look happy, just practiced. I go down into the basement and fish out the soccer player's folder. Arts and

Entertainment, Sports, Ball Games. It's not a very
thick folder, it just has a couple of articles about
his participation in championships, his selection as
Player of the Year, his divorce, the end of his playing
career, a failed commercial enterprise, duplicate
copies of articles relating to his time with Franziska.
I balance the papers in my hand, hesitate briefly,
and drop them in the recycling. It's never previously
occurred to me to remove anything from the archive.
It would have violated my professional ethos, I would
have felt like a swindler, a falsifier of history. But
what is there to keep me from doing such a thing
now that the archive belongs to me, represents my
world, is no one else's business, concerns no one else,
and no one bar me is permitted to look into it? In my
world, the soccer player no longer exists.

I looked out the folder of the singer with whom
Franziska had been together after the soccer player,
and drop that in the recycling as well. There
is nothing in the archive relating to the music
producer—he wasn't a person of public interest.

I feel more energized than I have for a long time,
I am afraid of my own past, and at the same time
I feel light as though a knot had burst that had
tethered me to this mountain of paper for decades.
If the archive is my world, then I can shape it as
I please, change it to suit myself. I walk through

the aisles, roll them forwards and back, pull out folders and set them aside. I get stuck at Politics and Political Ideologies. I draw out Fascism and National Socialism, Nationalism and after briefly hesitating, Communism as well. Socialism and Anarchism are permitted to stay, religiously inflected ideologies are out. I find Mussolini, Hitler, and Stalin in the section on European History, Twentieth Century, and they need to go as well. Ideally, I would destroy the folders, burn them so as never to have to look at them again, but I don't have a fireplace and don't trust myself to light a bonfire in the garden. There's always a neighbor who will complain or call the police. Besides, there's something comforting about the idea that even these monsters will remain in circulation, will be reused and become virgin paper for something new, for new thoughts, new people, a new history.

The recycling container is already half full, but I keep thinking of more subject categories and individuals that I want to evict from my world, Nuclear Weapons, Factory Farming, Sects and Cults, Anti-Semitism, Professional Sports and the imminent US Presidential Elections. That folder is still up in my office. I go up there, weigh it in my hand, and then suddenly feel unsure. There is no sense in randomly eliminating things and people, everything is connected to everything else, even the most inauspicious can lead to something valuable. If I throw away Fascism, then logic demands I remove Anti-Fascism as well, and with it all the heroic individuals who fought the Fascists. I need to reconsider the implications in detail, the consequences my purge would have. God didn't make the world in a day either.

Still, I won't take back today's activity, it feels like a purifying storm that has cleared a path in the archive, and I like the idea that it's no longer intact. Suddenly it seems to me as though escape might be possible, as though a fresh breeze is blowing through the holes in the archive.

The following day, I hear from Franziska. She doesn't write a lot, just that she'd be happy to see me. Her email seems oddly bland, as though a meeting with me is just one more commitment, like an interview, or a conference with her manager or her fans. She sent off her reply at 6:00 a.m., which surprises me. She used to be a late sleeper. When we stayed overnight somewhere after a concert, she never used to get up before ten o'clock, which sometimes led to arguments between us, as I always favored a quick getaway. You see, she said once, we'd just argue the whole time, we're really not compatible. I wonder what made her say that? It suggested she had entertained being in a relationship with me, perhaps even wished for it, only then to decide against it. Then why? Certainly not just because I was an early riser.

I have watched her sleeping. That too felt as weird as the idea of someone watching me sleep. I remember exactly, it was the night we spent in the same bed. When I woke up it was still dark, the only light in the room came from a security light on the parking lot outside. Franziska's face looked calm and somehow—I'm not sure how to put this—alien, neutral, as though it didn't belong to a person, but was just its own thing. I could feel the warmth from her body, smell the sourish, slightly metallic smell of her sleep. She lay there, half-covered, with the sheets jammed between her legs. I saw her frown, and she turned around, taking the cover with her. She lay there hunched over, facing away from me. Her T-shirt had ridden up, exposing her bare back, the little ridged line of her vertebrae. Lying there like that, she seemed terribly vulnerable, exposed. I pressed myself against her, to shield her, and, like that, fell asleep.

We are diving in murky water that seems to make our bodies look yellow and contourless against the green, we move rapidly and forcefully like giant fish, circle one another, without ever touching. Franziska beckons to me, turns away, disappears into the depths. I follow her into the darkness, but she is gone. I hang suspended in the black void, feeling myself becoming smaller and lesser. I roll myself up in a ball, I am a tiny throbbing creature with an enormous head and a tiny ridiculous body. I can feel Franziska's warmth, her heartbeat, which makes me shake all over, I am in her, a part of her, and yet separate from her.

I have to force myself not to write back straight-away. Instead, I pull out a folder and write on it *The Smell of Sleep*, and lay it on the little pile of empty folders that I've started. I go shopping, even though I have plenty to eat, then carry on down the hill, and up the riverbank, as I did on the first day. There's a little more water in it again, following the rain. I sit on the same bench I sat on on the day of my first walk, and try to imagine meeting Franziska, think about what to say to her, and how to say it. But all the while I'm thinking about her, I no longer feel the same love I did then, instead I feel confused, nervous, strangely empty. I half regret having written at all. The last time we spoke we were twenty-six; that's thirty years ago, half a lifetime. We were both failures, in our different ways; perhaps we were condemned to fail.

Back home, I write Franziska after all, more from a sense of duty than any confidence that our meeting could be a success and lead anywhere better than my memories. This time, she replies the same evening, and she sounds warmer than the first time, more personal. Where have you been all this time? she asks. She is living in a small place on Lake Zurich, one of those places where the local taxes are low, with the result that a lot of rich people live there who can't afford to stay in the city. You can tell she likes to cut to the chase, she suggests her house as the venue, and two o'clock on Wednesday as the time. We can sit in the garden, she writes, the forecast is good. I'm looking forward to seeing you again after such a long time. I don't know why, but I believe her.

*In order to distrac*t myself, I spend the next few days thinking about what folders I could remove, and what the consequences would be. I laid out large sheets of paper on my desk, and traced diagrams of what follows on from what, what is conditional on what. The task is an impossible one, the more I grapple with it, the more everything seems to be connected. Bad things lead on to good things, good things to bad. Any change in the structure has unpredictable consequences. Besides, I can't properly concentrate, I am continually thinking of Franziska and our upcoming meeting.

I have the irrational idea that she can feel me thinking of her. In fact, I've always believed in such a thing, that there is a connection between the actual Franziska and the one in my head, and that I am communing with Franziska at the moment I imagine her. How often I have loved her in my thoughts, have we loved each other, my Franziska and I.

She is standing up onstage with beating heart, shoots one last look in my direction, smiles, and sings a chanson by Barbara or Jacques Brel. "Dis, quand reviendras-tu?" Each time she sings that particular song, I imagine she is thinking of me, standing in the wings, lurking behind the curtain, softly mouthing the words to myself.

> *Day and night I see your face in front of me*
> *I'm sick with love and long for thee...*

Two years after I broke up with my archive colleague, my mother died, and even though I hadn't had much contact with her lately, her death changed a lot of things for me. I started to think about my own life and death, after not having given them much thought at all. It's as though my mother had left me not only the house and all her possessions, but also the responsibility for myself. She had carried me into the world, brought me up, now she had preceded me out of it. And now that she was no longer there, I lost all orientation, as after sunset when it's dark, and the compass points are no longer clear to see. I rarely thought of Franziska at this time, she was with her singer, apparently unreachable, and increasingly just an image, getting paler and less distinct.

I had various health problems, nothing serious, presumably all psychosomatic in origin, various aches and pains, chronic fatigue, lack of appetite. I felt tired, demotivated, depressed. For a time, I was doing so badly that I could barely muster the energy to go to work in the morning, to eat regularly, to pursue my physical hygiene. Everyday things, self-evident things, suddenly struck me as bizarre, I didn't know my own face in the mirror, the simplest actions perturbed me. I would do something and simultaneously watch myself doing it, and wonder what I was doing it for, and not something else, or nothing at all. I was caught up in endless conversations with myself, that, come to think of it, I've been engaged in for all my life. I offer commentary and disagreement, explain things to myself, describe predicaments, and enact them, play different parts, manipulate experiences,

reinforce myself in my conclusions, apologize for my
failures, console myself for losses. I am my own best
friend, but what goes on in my head isn't a dialog,
even if there are several voices speaking, it's a dismal
monolog.

Come to me, says Franziska. She wants to comfort
me, takes me in her arms, strokes my head, there,
there. Maybe you've been working too hard. But
it's not Franziska, it's me, trying to comfort myself.
I feel as though I can see my features behind hers,
disfiguring them, it's an image as from a horror film,
where the mask slips and it suddenly becomes clear
that the victim is in fact the attacker.

The dominant feeling of that time—as only dawns
on me now that it's over—was fear, a fear that kept
growing until I was afraid it would drive me insane.
I thought of getting help, having myself booked into
a clinic, and I might have done so, if I hadn't felt that
not even that would help me escape from my own
clutches.

This condition lasted for almost a whole year,
until suddenly, for no external reason, it stopped.
One morning I got up and knew I was over the worst.
I showered and went to work, did the housework in
the evening, and finally gave some attention to the
paperwork the inheritance had brought in its train. It
was about that time too that I decided to move into

my mother's house, and not sell it as I'd thought I would—but never did anything toward realizing.

I had been in the house for a while now. I was doing better but was increasingly withdrawn. I no longer had any time for my few remaining friends, went out even less than before, instead busied myself with the garden in my free time, where there was always something to do, even though nothing changed. I was in my mid-forties, but I was basically reconciled to the fact that there wasn't going to be anything new in my life from here on in. All around me, I could see men taking up marathon running, or buying themselves sleek cars or showing themselves with much younger women on their arms, and I felt nothing but pity for them, pity and contempt.

For the twenty-fifth anniversary of our high school graduation, a few of my erstwhile classmates had gotten it into their heads to organize a class reunion. It began with a letter asking us to supply addresses for some long-missing members of the group. I ignored the letter, I had long since lost contact with everyone in the class, then a month later, there was a second letter, saying all the addresses had now been traced, and a program was being put together, and we were invited to meet at

such and such a time on such and such a date at a
country inn, there was a note on how to get there,
and a choice of two menus, one vegetarian, the other
not. Along with the letter was a list of addresses
and phone numbers for the entire class; next to
Fabienne's was the address and phone number of an
agency. I ignored this second letter as well.

One evening, about two weeks before the planned
reunion, the phone rang. The noisy jangling sound
made me jump, I hardly ever got any calls, and
had almost forgotten its existence. It was the class
member who had been the driving force behind
the reunion. She gave me a boisterous greeting and
said she hadn't yet received my acceptance. The
call was unpleasant to me. It hadn't cost me any
effort to ignore the invitation, but now with my
classmate on the phone, it seemed impolite to me to
refuse without giving a good reason. She seemed so
thoroughly taken with her plan. Everyone's coming,
she said, of course bar the two or three who've died.

She told me about them, one had had a long
dependency on drugs and had died three years ago,
the other had died in a climbing accident in the Alps.
I couldn't match faces to their names, but I didn't
ask and just said how awful and that I was sorry, but
I couldn't make the agreed date. My old classmate
was silent for a moment, then she played her trump

card and said: Fabienne is coming. Who? I asked. Fabienne, she repeated and laughed. You must mean Franziska, I said. If you prefer, she said, you used to be so close. I never liked it when people stick their noses in what I do and don't do. Those clones of me in others' heads, they're nothing to do with me, and yet they threaten me too, they look like me, they imitate my voice, they do things I would never do, but which as possibilities become part of my life. I know you much better than you know yourself, which of my partners once said that to me? The claim made me simultaneously furious and helpless. How could I reply?

Perhaps Fabienne will even agree to sing for us, said my old classmate. I promised to check my diary. A few days later, I agreed to go.

Franziska wasn't there. I only learned that after I'd arrived. A few of my old classmates, sitting outside the country inn, smoking, hailed me with remarks about my appearance and how I supposedly hadn't changed a bit. Contrary to my expectations, I was able to place them right away, and remembered how even when we were all at school, I had detested them.

The evening hadn't properly gotten going, and I was thoroughly regretting that I'd come.

The organizer stepped out of the inn. She too was little changed. She kissed me on both cheeks, then looked at me with a fake sad expression and said, unfortunately Fabienne wasn't able to make it. She had agreed to fill in at the last moment for another artiste who had gotten sick and was very sorry not to be here with us. The excuse sounded every bit as implausible as the classmate's show of disappointment. I should have left there and then, but that would have drawn everyone's attention to me still more, so I followed her inside, where there was more exclaiming and shaking of hands and kissing of cheeks.

Franziska was the main subject that evening, and the longer it went on, the more disrespectful the tone of the remarks about her. Even then she had thought she was better than everyone else, apparently. Her music was so dire, she could only keep her career going by continually turning up with new partners in the yellow press, that sort of thing. I should have intervened on her behalf, but I've never been much of a fighter, and I just kept my mouth shut. There was only one woman, who had been Franziska's best friend at school and later went to nursing college with her, who countered the gossip. She looked very upset as she spoke, and continually looked over in my direction, as though expecting me to chime in.

Although I'd driven there, I had a lot to drink that night. When I got up to go to the men's room at one stage, I noticed how far gone I was, and stepped out for some air. It was pitch-black, in the middle distance I could hear cowbells and the rustling of a stream. The inn had been a mill in former times and stood all by itself in the landscape. In front were a few metal tables and chairs and I sat down. I wondered how I was going to get home. It would be irresponsible to drive, but I really didn't fancy getting a ride with any of these people.

The door opened, a split of light fell on the yard, and shortly after, Franziska's defender joined me at my table and lit a cigarette. Do you want one? she asked and held out the pack. I shook my head. We're the only ones here to keep faith with Fabienne, she said, her only real friends in that whole bunch. Are you in touch with her? I asked. Yes, she said, we meet from time to time, not all that often, she's on the road so much. Sometimes I look after the house when she's away. When we see each other, we talk about old times, we've talked about you too sometimes.

I wanted to ask her what Franziska had said about me, but I let it go. She was the only reason I came tonight, I said. Shall we go? suggested Franziska's friend. Can you take me? I asked. I said I was too drunk, but if she was happy to drive, we could take my car.

Her school friend was not at all like Franziska, but their closeness in my eyes gave her a strange luster. She pulled up in front of the tenement where she lived.

How will you get home now? she asked. I could sleep in the car, I suppose, I said, or else I'll leave it here and walk. It must be more than an hour on foot, she said, and laughed. She hesitated, then said, Why don't you come up. I've got my son living with me, but I'm sure he's not back yet. He's always out clubbing at weekends.

The apartment was cold and smelled of cold cigarette smoke. We stood in the kitchen and drank a glass of red wine, also far too cold. I shouldn't have left it in the fridge, she said, but I don't drink much during the week. And I don't have male company either. She laughed nervously. Are you always this quiet?

Had I been in love with Franziska at the time, she wanted to know, had there ever been anything between us? It's all a long time ago, I said evasively. What does she say? You know what she's like, she replied. We were always in love with other people. Weren't you?

After we'd kissed, she said it was odd, absurd in fact, but she felt guilty. You could rub my back. She pulled her jersey over her head and turned away from me. Come on, she said, leading the way to her bedroom, and lying down on the bed.

Following that first night, we never talked about Franziska again, but even so I had the feeling I was closer to her when we were together. From that time on, we would meet up every two or three weeks. I never had her back to my house, but she would phone when her son was staying at his girlfriend's or was away for some other reason. We would have a snack, sleep together, and I went home. It was the most uncomplicated relationship I had ever had, presumably because we liked each other, but weren't in love. Each demanded nothing of the other, not even fidelity. I don't think she had anyone else at the time, but I never asked. To be honest, I wasn't interested, just as the rest of her life didn't interest me, and yet I listened to her gratefully when she told me about it. That gave me the feeling I was a part of it, like a distant relative who is just a name to the others, and yet belongs to the family.

Sometimes she told me stories from the hospital where she worked or she complained about trouble with her son, who was fed up with his traineeship and wanted to quit. But why am I telling you this?

she would say, you're not my therapist. Then she talked about her ex-husband, who kept bothering her, even though she'd told him a thousand times she was finished with him. In the tenement where she lived, an elevator had been installed, with no end of noise and dirt. Now the owner wanted more rent, even though she lived on the ground floor, and never used it. Her boss was being sued for medical malpractice, which she frankly thought he deserved. Her son had a new girlfriend, a really sweet girl, and she hoped this time it would work out for him. She talked and talked, then we would sleep together again, and eventually she said I ought to go, she needed to get some sleep, she had a busy day tomorrow. I lay in bed and watched her get dressed. She had the habit of putting on her bra first and then her slip, which I found strangely arousing. Then she walked around the apartment in her underwear, cleared the dishes into the dishwasher, picked her clothes off the living room floor, until I too finally got up and dressed.

I'll find my own way out. She laughed and kissed me on the mouth. Have you seen Franziska again? I asked, pulling her to me one last time. I'd be grateful if you wouldn't tell her about us.

Our relationship went on for six years and could have gone on for longer. But at that point I lost my job and fell into a deep hole. I canceled on my girlfriend a couple of times, and after the third time she asked if I still wanted to see her. I said my life was a bit of a mess, and what I needed just then was time alone. She was quiet for a moment, then said, well, call me when you want to see me again. I'd miss our meetings, myself.

The fact that I then didn't call her wasn't down to any decision on my part, I just kept putting it off and putting it off, until it would have felt weird if I'd gotten in touch.

What am I going to talk about with Franziska? Will we tell each other our life stories? But I know hers from the newspapers, and there's not much to say about mine. Will we find our way back into the ease with which we once used to talk about everything under the sun? Generally, I prefer silence to speech. Will we talk about the state of the world? Current events? Climate change? What would be the point of that? Her views won't be any more trenchant than mine, or those of the newspaper commentary pages. What's the point of trying to see Franziska at all?

I always liked the idea of seeing her again after decades: converse, embrace, maybe more. I was wary of imagining such a meeting in too much detail. Now that it's absolutely imminent, I find I'm afraid of it.

There are a hundred ways for it to go wrong, and I can't imagine how it would go right.

Two days before the due date, I take my car around to the mechanic. I haven't used it for a long time, and am relieved it still starts. When I'm talking to the mechanic, I realize how out of the habit of talking to people I really am.

The car's ready for me the next day, and instead of taking it home from the garage, I go for a drive in it. Quite without intending such a thing, I find myself near the small lake where Franziska and I went swimming a few times. The public baths don't open until early summer, there's a single car in the parking lot, but no one around. Perhaps it belongs to a bird-watcher or dog walker or something. It's overcast, but not cold.

The entrance to the baths is open, so I wander down to the lake. Everything looks the way it did then, the old wooden changing rooms, the kiosk and the fire pit, the shallow children's pond ringed with logs, the swimming raft bobbing around a little way out.

I bend down and feel the temperature of the water; it's warmer than I expected. I look around; there's still no one to be seen. I strip off and walk into the water, stark naked. I stand around for a long time, up to my hips, then launch myself forward. The cold briefly takes my breath away. I swim out a bit. If I were suddenly to lose consciousness, no one could help me, and I would go under. I dip my head in the water, keeping my eyes open. It's very quiet. The lake is clearer now than it is in summer, but I still don't see much except for light, altering the color of the water, a few tendrils of aquatic plants, the algae-grown chain that secures the raft, the shadow of the raft on the lake bottom, my pallid body against the greenish water.

Eventually, it is said, drowned bodies bob up to the surface. Where does one learn such things? And does it take days? Weeks? The dead in my own life bob up, my parents, my grandparents, my two dead classmates, and other, remoter persons I can't recognize, stiff cadavers slowly rising through the water. They look eerie, uncanny, but I am not afraid of them, I know them, and they are part of me.

I return to the surface, gasping, and swim back to the shore. I didn't bring a towel and so I lie down on the grass, but it's so cold I finally have to get my clothes on before I'm dry.

When I get to the car, I see Franziska standing there, as though she'd been waiting for me. She smiles, nods, and starts down the gravel path. After

two or three hundred yards she takes a boardwalk
that leads across a reedbed to a wooden viewing
platform for bird-watchers. She climbs the steep
steps, and I follow. When I get to the top, Fabienne
is leaning on the railing, looking out across the
lake. Her shoulders are a little hunched, as though
she is cold or perhaps apprehensive. I stand close
behind her and lay my hands on her shoulders. Her
head inclines forward. I take her by the hips, push
my hands under her anorak. She straightens up,
otherwise barely moves. I kiss her neck, stroke her
breasts. She turns. When I make to kiss her lips, she
turns her head.

In the last few days, I must have checked the
map half a dozen times to see what the best way is
to Franziska's village, and even then I get lost in the
unfamiliar Oberland, where everywhere looks the
same to me. The roads are almost empty, there are
very few cars out, and even the little settlements look
deserted. There are a few old people out and about,
all of them alone, they look to me as though they're
searching for something whose existence they no
longer quite believe in.

I've allowed myself too much time for the drive,
and in spite of losing my way and endless detours, I'm

an hour early. Just before the place itself, I stop at a wooded roadside on the heights. Franziska's village is below me, the walk to her house won't be more than a few minutes.

There is a wonderful view of the lake and the opposite shore, and beyond, the chains of hills and then mountains whose peaks are lost in the clouds. There are pop-up thunderstorms predicted for the mountains, which is unusual for the time of year.

I'm nervous, and my tummy is growling. I've brought nothing to read. In the glove compartment I find an instruction manual for the car, from which I learn a few things I'd never have guessed. If, in unlocking the car, you keep your finger on the window steering, then all the windows will open at once. The things these engineers come up with. I test it out, and it's true.

I leave the car and walk along the roadside a little way. Every hundred yards or so, there's a wooden bench. Some of the benches have little signs, memorials or dedications to someone or other, it seems this is an orphanage for wooden benches up here. For Gerda on her 75th birthday. To Astrid and Roland on their golden wedding anniversary. For Franziska, love of my life. I imagine her walking along the wood's edge, sitting down, and thinking of me, as I now think of her.

The garden is surrounded by a high hedge, from
the road you can't see anything but the hedge and the
entrance. The rest of the house has the effect of being
out of focus, or out of range, as though shrouded in
invisible fog. I stay in the car a moment, then, on
the dot of the appointed time, press the doorbell.
As though Franziska had been lurking behind the
door, it opens immediately, and we stand face-to-face,
quite speechless to begin with. Franziska looks utterly
unchanged, it's not possible that she can still look so
young. She smiles, and says come in. She turns on
her heel and leads the way through a bright entrance
hall into a large living room. The décor is tasteful,
one can tell that the furniture didn't come cheap, but
also that it was chosen and assembled professionally
and by someone who doesn't live here. The room
has something impersonal, almost sterile, it's a
little like walking through a catalog. On a low glass-
topped table is a tray with an empty carafe, glasses, a
coffeepot, and two cups. Would you like coffee? asks
Franziska. She seems as bashful as me but can deal
with it better. I nod, yes please. She leans forward
to fill two cups, but no coffee flows from the pot.
Her hand shakes a little. Black and no sugar, isn't
that right? Yes, I say, you remember that? And you

take plenty of milk. And no sugar, she says, at my age you have to watch your weight. She pours some invisible milk into her cup. You look just ravishing, you haven't changed at all. Nor have you. I look at my hands, holding the empty cup, indeed, they seem to look much more youthful than I remember them looking. We're both talking nothing but nonsense, presumably we've noticed, and have fallen silent. After a while, Franziska asks me: Would you like me to show you the house? She hasn't touched her coffee.

She leads me through the house as an estate agent might show a potential purchaser, remarks on the good points, lists the en suites and guest bathrooms. The house was built in the sixties, which makes it older than we are. But everything has been diligently kept up and improved, the cavity walls and roof are insulated. Would she really have said cavity walls? My study, my library, my bedroom. The guest bedroom. Here I keep all sorts of junk, old clothes, tax files, records. If you'd like a copy of a CD, just tell me, I've plenty here. I've had a little studio installed in the basement where I sometimes go to record. No, I don't look after the garden myself, there's a gardener who comes and does it every week. I've no idea what tree that is, it must be older than the house. A sugar maple? The pool is ten meters, there's a heat pump that warms the water.

I swam in our lake yesterday, I tell her. Which is our lake? she asks. The one we always used to go to, don't you remember? Oh, yes, she says. Did we go that often? I haven't swum in a lake in years. I'm always afraid someone will take pictures of me in my bathing suit and sell them. We stand silently beside the pool, probably we both thought our meeting would be different.

Yes, says Franziska, my first love was you. I can hardly believe you weren't aware of it. She speaks in a monotone, as though reading from a text she doesn't understand. The time we shared a room in the Black Forest, the time I asked you to stay with me in Chur. We kiss, but it feels as though I'm kissing empty space. I look at my watch. It's only two o'clock.

On my way home, I'm thinking what am I going to tell Franziska. I could claim I suddenly felt unwell, that I hadn't found the house, I could just apologize without giving a reason. Maybe she wouldn't even answer. She must get loads of letters and emails from people who are after something.

Before driving off, I had closed all the shutters, as though I was going on a journey and wouldn't be back for a long time. The house is shady and cooler than usual. Everything is where I left it, and why wouldn't it be. Then I am suddenly bothered by the origami zoo. I'm really not one of those crazies that you read about in the paper who sit in their stuffed-full houses doing crazy things, not talking to anyone, and living off soup packets and rusks. And whose bodies are found, weeks after their death, and the neighbors all say, who would have thought it, he was so quiet, a friendly private man.

What would my neighbors say about me? They don't know me any better than I know them. Over time, most of the houses were sold off or inherited, new people have moved in, I haven't gone out of my way to get to know them. I greet them when they greet me, I don't know their names. I fetch a broom and sweep up the entire menagerie and throw it in the bin where it belongs.

The house seems very empty to me, emptier than ever before. I try to think of Franziska, but she's gone, leaving behind another name, Fabienne, and a bland picture that might have appeared in the press, and a kiss into fresh air. You did want to see me, didn't you? You only agreed out of kindness, because you didn't want to appear arrogant. She doesn't reply. She smiles. But the smile on her face is not for me, it's the frozen publicity smile that she has mastered so well.

I sit at my computer, with an empty email addressed to Franziska on the screen. I don't know what to say to her. Maybe it's better not to write at all. She'll understand and feel secretly relieved.

It's gotten dark. I am still sitting in front of the computer, the screen has gone dark. Then the telephone rouses me from my thoughts. Three, four, five rings. Unknown caller, it says on the display. Finally I accept the call and say my name. Why didn't you come? I hear Franziska's voice. She sounds just the same, maybe the timbre is a little lower, but the voice is still the same. We had a date, she said, did you forget?

I don't know what to say. I was there, I say, only far too early. I parked by the side of the wood over the village. You have an amazing view. Franziska laughs. And so you thought, well, I've taken in the view, may as well go now? I could have told you the names of all the peaks, I know them all. Like my grandfather, I say, he could do that too. I hope that's the only thing I have in common with him. He was a kindly man, I say.

The conversation develops quite effortlessly. For weeks, for months now, I haven't exchanged more than a couple of sentences with anyone, but Franziska helps me out. She says she understands me. I must have thought I was pressuring her. It was true, she got all sorts of letters. People writing me their heartbreak, asking for advice, teachers coming up with grammatical mistakes in my lyrics, people offering me investment ins, men I've never heard of declaring their undying love. That was more or less what I had in mind, I say. Franziska laughs easily. You tried to do that once before.

We must have spoken for two hours. My ear is hot from the pressure. While we're speaking, I walk around the house, and it feels to me as though Franziska is walking at my side, being shown my cheerless life. At the same time, I have the feeling as though everything there is someone else's, it's not my house, and I look at the furniture, the paintings, the photographs as though they all belonged to some stranger. But we don't talk about that. We talk almost exclusively about old times, and we laugh, I haven't laughed as much in the whole of last year as I did in those two hours.

It's astonishing how much Franziska remembers, some things she remembers better than I do, or she remembers them differently. It feels as though we've only just seen each other, she says. You're right, I say, that's how it feels to me too. You haven't changed a bit. You're only saying that because I'm not in front of you now. She laughs, and then groans a little. What is it? I ask. Each time I laugh, I get a pain in my back, she says, laughing again, it's just we're getting old, and when things stop hurting, then it's because we're dead. Eventually she says she has to go to bed, she needs her beauty sleep. Will you be home tomorrow? I'm always home. Well, let's talk again then. There's so much more to say. I'll call you.

I would like to go for a walk, my walks have become an integral part of my days, but I daren't leave the house in case I miss Franziska's call. I spend the whole day glued to the window, watching. But there's hardly anything to look at. A woman passes pushing a baby carriage.

Yesterday's conversation left me feeling strangely euphoric, even though we didn't do anything but reminisce. Franziska and I could be friends again, could see each other, I could accompany her to her concerts, wait for her backstage, keep the fans off her and later drink a glass of wine with her in a hotel bar in some medium-sized city. What more could I want? But the longer she doesn't ring, the more agitated I become. At concerts she's bound to be besieged by swarms of people, I would only get between her and her fans. And who's to say that she doesn't have a friend or lover anyway? Men probably queue up to see her or be seen with her. She's beautiful, she's successful, she has money. To appear in public with me must be an awful notion to her, embarrassing. Who is the new man at Fabienne's side? An unemployed archivist, a sociopathic eccentric. No one's ever heard of him. And those clothes! The haircut! What a positively grotesque couple!

I do my laundry, so as to distract myself. Half my socks have holes, my shirt collars are worn, my pants are shiny and frayed. I never minded what I looked like, I took a minimum of care over my appearance, just enough not to attract attention, to disappear in a crowd, to be invisible. Now I'm ashamed of the way I look. I fish out a shirt and a pair of pants in decent repair, and drape them both on hangers in my closet, my costume for an appearance that may never happen.

It's not until evening that the call comes. Hallo, Franziska says after I pick up and say my name. Her voice sounds close, much closer than it did yesterday. What were you up to just now? Waiting for your call, I say, trying not to make it sound like a reproach. I'm sorry, she says, I should have told you I couldn't manage before evening. I was in town all day.

The thought of her doing things, running around, meeting people, offends me. I would have wished her to be sitting at home all day, as I was, thinking about me, and looking forward to our conversation, imagining it, planning what she was going to say.

I don't want to cramp you, I say, what you do is none of my business. She laughs in astonishment and asks, Why do you say that? in a puzzled tone.

Now she's bound to take me for a madman, a stalker who wants to know everything there is to know about her, observes her, and will be a problem unless she brushes him off smartly.

Sorry, I say, I'm just talking nonsense. Maybe I've been thinking about us too much. About us, she says, that sounds strange. And what are you up to? I ask, to change the subject. I have a pool, she says. Is that an activity? Don't be like that, she says, I mean, I'm sitting by the pool, having a drink, and chatting with a friend. I wonder if she's in her bathing suit, but I don't trust myself to ask.

This time our conversation is more serious, and less fluent, sometimes there are long silences, we don't know what to say next. Franziska tells me about her concert tours, but I can't shake the feeling that we're actually talking about something else, that this other subject is the key to our conversation, and our words are just overtones or side notes.

After the bungled opening, I don't trust myself to ask Franziska what she's doing in her life, if she's working on a recording, has other projects, is planning a tour, is going steady with someone. It's strange, she says, you're the only person to call me Franziska, not even my parents still call me that. And it was you who came up with my recording name. Do you want me to call you Fabienne, then? No, no, she says quickly, I'm Franziska to you, and that's how it should stay. What does she mean by that? That I should stay in the past tense, where I belong? That Fabienne is nothing to do with me? That the girl I swore love to hasn't existed now for a long time?

At the end of maybe an hour, Franziska says she's tired, it had been a long day. There's silence. Shall we talk again tomorrow? I ask uncertainly. Tomorrow or the day after, she says, and I won't call before eight. I don't want you to sit around at home all day waiting. She laughs again. I wasn't going to go anywhere, I say. Sleep tight, she says.

Franziska calls the next day. This time, she's full of questions, she wants to know what I've done with myself in all the time we didn't see each other. It sounds a bit as though she's prepared this time, like an interviewer. I ask myself, why. What does she want? What would she like to hear? Why is she even interested? I don't know how to answer her questions.

When I tell her about my job, she asks me if it was interesting work. I never asked myself that, I say, and have to laugh, truly not. On leaving college, I was pleased to have a job to go to, and I enjoyed doing the work. It wasn't strenuous, and it was varied and fairly well paid. It probably wasn't really interesting, though. It didn't involve making anything new, just ordering and classifying the work of others.

I would like to tell her about the Present One, about God the Archivist, who keeps our files up to date, not to sit in judgment over us, but just to see that nothing gets lost. The universe as one huge archive, that exists purely to represent itself, an infinite web of things and beings and events that are all connected to one another, and within it, the pair of us, completely without significance, but at least not alone.

Are you still there? asks Franziska. I'm sure you had a lot do with people, she prompts me. Not so much, I say. They gave us instructions, which we carried out. But now it's all done electronically. The journalists are able to find the material they're looking for by themselves. Archivists are on the way out. She asks me what I'm doing now, what my plans are—questions I'd dreaded. I say, at the moment I don't have a job. I avoid the word *unemployed*. I am working, and it was my own decision not to look for another job.

I tell Franziska about the archive in my basement, even though, to me now talking about it, it sounds as crazy as it must to her hearing about it. And she does seem slightly dumbstruck. It's like a huge treasure trove, I say, a world unto itself, this archive has had tens of thousands of hours of labor expended upon it. My mother used to collect everything she could find about me, says Franziska, every review, every profile, every concert listing. Some time, when she was quite old, she gave it all to me, a huge cardboard box full. I got it carried up to the attic. She seems to want to say something more, but she hesitates before going on. Would you like to have it? A file on your life? I wanted to make something like that, I say, but then I didn't. Whatever I put into it, it would have been too much and too little. I often thought about it in the last few weeks, my life, more than I ever did, I read and sorted old correspondence, looked at photographs, remembered, but I'm not sure whether it did me any good, whether it helped me any. It had the effect of churning up the sediment, now I'm sitting in the murk and can't see anything.

After that, it's my turn to hesitate. Franziska groans again, as during our first call. My back, she says, it's nothing. Don't you have any aches and pains? You're no younger than I am. I stopped running the archive, I say. A couple of weeks ago. Just like that? she asks. Yes, just like that. I still don't know what I'm going to do with all the files. Maybe I'll just throw them all out. And all my old stuff, letters, photographs, notes. Then what will you do? asks Franziska. She sounds concerned. Start something completely different.

My words are quicker than my thoughts. I haven't given any serious thought to what I'll do next, but I would be ashamed to admit as much to Franziska. That sounds exciting, says Franziska. I feel jealous. But she also says, I shouldn't be too quick to wind up the archive. I'd like to see it, will you show it to me sometime? Of course, I say, you can visit me whenever you like. But there's no view of mountains from here. Just mountains of paper, says Franziska and laughs, watch out, I'll really come. Then she suggests things I might want to do, like open a bar or learn to play the piano so that I can accompany her on tour. You could study theology, she says. Why would I do that? Ministers are in short supply, and they are well paid. Or become a teacher, they're always in demand. I don't have to decide today, do I? I say. Or stockbroker, says Franziska, or you breed chickens or pigeons in your back garden.

And what are you doing these days? I ask, to put a stop to the stream of suggestions. There's been nothing about you in the papers for ages. Have you got a file on me? Of course, I say, it wasn't even my idea. You're a public personage. I wish I weren't, she says, and sighs. But it's up to you whether you are or not. Up to a point that's true, she says. I can keep journalists from entering my house or standing outside the church when I get married, but I can't do anything to prevent them from reporting or speculating about me. But you never married, I say.

I tried to keep it all under control, she says. When I gave interviews, I insisted on reading what I'm supposed to have said, though it didn't always happen that way. There wasn't much more I could do.

Franziska stands between the shelves, takes down a file, reads the title, puts it back, takes out another one, Human Anatomy, Cytology, Histology, Human Physiology, Personal Well-Being and Security, Toxicology. Do you know all those classifications by heart? Most of them, I say. After so many years. But there are some subject areas that don't come up very frequently. Or that drop out of fashion and fall into obscurity. Do you remember Chaos Theory? In the nineties that was all the rage. Mandelbrot fractals, the butterfly that flaps its wing and starts a storm.

No one's interested in that anymore. Cybernetics, Nanotechnology. Now they're all talking about AI, but that'll quiet down too after a while.

Franziska steps out of an aisle, turns the wheel to move the shelving. The weight of the world, she says, as the shelf collides with its neighbor with a dull thump. She enters the newly created space, picks up the pile of empty folders lying there. The Sounds of Water, the Sounds of Birds in Flight, the Smell of Sleep, the Noonday Demons. Is there nothing to be said about those?

Those are new files that I started, but I don't know where they should go or what I'm going to put in them, I say. That's the problem with any organizational system, there's always a lot that won't fit into it, and slips through the cracks. Case in point, the Sounds of Water, she says, and opens the folder. But there's nothing in it. It's not empty, though, I say. I always imagine these folders are full, only not with writing. This one contains all the sounds of water. Can you hear them? And where have you filed me? asks Franziska, putting the folders down. Your file is upstairs, I say, I was looking at it lately.

Then Franziska suddenly has her file in her hands, opens it out, and leafs through it. My life, she says, and laughs, but it's all just paper, nothing but words. She brushes her hand across the clippings, wipes away the writing like a layer of dust, so that all that remains is blank paper, yellowed, stained, creased, sometimes torn paper. She closes the folder, puts it away, and steps up to me very close. That's not me, she says, the person you have in your file. Not a word in there is true, not a photograph. That's not me. I am that I am. She laughs. I am the one who is always present.

That night, we are again swimming in the lake together, Franziska beckons me down to the depths, deeper than ever before. We spiral down into utter darkness, she dodges my kisses, smiles, come with me. Eventually we will have dived so far down that I will be unable to reach the surface again. By morning, I am sweaty and exhausted, as though I hadn't slept a wink.

Your first boyfriend, I say. Today, Franziska didn't call until ten o'clock, I'd almost given up waiting. The one you refused to even name to the journalists. Who was it? There's silence, I'm not sure whether it's that Franziska's thinking or is unwilling to answer. Was it me? I ask, following up. I only made him up to be left in peace, she says, finally. But if he had existed, he would have been you. You're not the first to ask, by the way.

Anita had asked as well. And told Franziska about our relationship. Why did you finish with her? she asks. I didn't finish with her, it was only ever an affair, I say. Quite a protracted affair, may I say. I say I felt guilty about it throughout. I was never in love with her, and I don't think she was with me either. What makes you so sure about that? asks Franziska. Did you ever tell a woman you loved her? You would know that better than anyone, I say. That was forty years ago, we were both children. We were in love with a different person every week. Not me, I was only ever in love with you. Anyway, it was thirty-nine years ago. And you've not said it to a woman since then?

This would be the moment to tell Franziska my love, but I don't. She suddenly seems very alien to me, and I'm annoyed by her question and the criticism implicit in it. Would I even recognize her if we met?

Maybe I just didn't have the confidence after that, I say. A declaration of love isn't a marriage proposal, says Franziska. I have to think about the interview she gave with the soccer player, where she said she didn't believe in love at first sight, but that she felt great love for her new partner. And did you tell each of your men that you loved them? And loved them all, the producer and the soccer player and the singer and God knows who else? Yes, says Franziska, sounding very cool, I loved them all and I told them so. And sooner or later it was over. It was only me you were never able to tell that to. She laughs. What do you know about my life anyway? Do you really believe the stuff from magazines that's in your files? Life isn't paper, you know. She starts singing, her voice mocking:

Si tu ne comprends pas qu'il te faut revenir
Je ferai de nous deux mes plus beaux souvenirs
Je reprendrai ma route, le monde m'émerveille
J'irai me réchauffer à un autre soleil
Je ne suis pas de celles qui meurent de chagrin
Je n'ai pas la vertu des femmes de marins...

There's a long silence, then Franziska says, you can't get back lost time, you ought to know that. Sleep well. And before I can reply, she has hung up.

Franziska hasn't called again, and I can't say I blame her. I would like to call her to apologize, but I never asked her for her number, and it never said anything other than Unknown Caller on my display. I sit around all day at home, not doing anything, not even running to fetch the newspapers out of

the mailbox before it bursts. I don't do anything in
the house or the garden, I feel disabled. The only
thing I still do is walk. I walk along the river, and
try to retrieve my memories of Franziska, to think
of her as I used to do; but the glossy pictures from
the file get in the way of my memories of our time
together, and I keep hearing the mocking words that
Franziska sang to me on the occasion of our last call.
I will warm myself at another sun, I am not of the
company of those who die of broken hearts, I am not
as virtuous as a sailor's wife.

It feels to me as though she has turned me down
a second time, in a sense renewing her rejection the
way some people renew their vows.

The whole world seems changed, the sky seems
broader, the air clearer, the colors more distinct.
Even the sounds seem louder now, and with an edge
of menace. It's almost like my first walk two months
ago, when the fullness of my sensations intoxicated
and terrorized me.

Today on the riverbank, I have to think how
in all the happiest moments of my life I was always
alone. It's a sorry thought, really. But why? Because
I was self-sufficient? When I was young, I used to
read a lot, I lived more in fantasy than reality. By

now I make my own world. My imagination has given me everything I wanted. Reality just couldn't compete. There was always a little vestige of doubt whether I had made a pact with the devil, whether this imaginary life would satisfy me where everything was easy for me, where Franziska loved me, where we were together. There were always moments of clarity, as today, down by the river, where I guessed that reality could be much richer and more intense than any fantasy. Those are the happiest, and at the same time the gloomiest moments of my life, happiness that feels like unhappiness, or unhappiness that feels like happiness. It's all the same. Then it dawns on me what life might be like, but also how little I have opened myself to it. Would anyone miss me if I didn't exist? The few people who send me birthday cards or Christmas cards? Not even them. If they happen to catch my death announcement, in their last thought of me they will strike out my name on their card index, and then it will be as though I had never been. I was always just the one who was present. I was present where I was always present. I am that I am. A blank.

This week it rains so hard and so incessantly that there's no possibility of walking. To get away from the empty house, I take the car and drive around aimlessly. Sometimes I stop between two localities, pull over to the side of the road or the opening of a track, and stare out into the landscape. I switch off the windshield wipers, and the rain enfolds me. One time, I realize I'm quite close to Franziska's home. Again, I'm parked on the roadside, looking down at the lake. The mountains are obscured by clouds, which themselves resemble a continually changing mountain range, an accelerated version of the time that makes and unmakes mountains.

I think of the people who used to live here eons ago, our oldest ancestors who came here from God knows where and built houses on stilts by the side of the lake. They fished, they hunted in the forests, they collected mushrooms and berries. They wove cloth and made pots and tools of surprising quality and beauty. They put up provisions for the winter. They must have worried if they had enough food, if the snow would come early and make it impossible for them to collect firewood. How terrible the world must have been then, and how beautiful, when everything was just what it was, a hut, a fire pit, a millstone, an earthenware pot, a fishing net.

A few years ago, in the course of an excavation near the lakeshore, the skeleton of a young woman was unearthed, who had drowned some six thousand years ago, she moved me more than all the usual finds of tools and weapons and potsherds. Perhaps she had gone swimming like Franziska and me, perhaps with her lover, or in thoughts of him. She must have had a name, a family, a life. She was obstinate or gentle or passionate. Perhaps she was beautiful. In the newspaper there was a photograph of her skull, which is probably now in some research center or museum, all that's left of her, nothing.

I drive on, stop outside Franziska's house. It looks just the way I imagined, only perhaps a little smaller, and a little run-down. Is it possible I saw a picture of it somewhere? Or did Anita describe it to me? It's true, from the street you do only see the entrance, and a tall yew hedge. I picture Franziska at one of the windows, catching sight of me, and beckoning to me. She is standing in the doorway, barefoot and in some sort of kimono. I'm sorry, she says, I really didn't want to hurt you. I'm really sorry. She shakes her head, looks down at the floor, and I step up to her and take her in my arms. We stand there like that for a long time, I feel the warmth of her body through the silky material, her hair in my face. The rain spills down...I must stop, I've just been speaking aloud, and the sound of my voice has startled me. I must stop this.

———

I am sitting in the car, the world around me is blurred with rain running down the windshield. The windows are misted on the inside, and I crack open the side window. The drumming of the rain on the car roof, the bright glugging of the water streaming down the street in little rivulets, the gurgle as it disappears down the drain. The hissing of the traffic from the nearby through-road. A deep growl, and periodic hissing and juddering, the refuse collection is going by, two men in orange waterproofs tossing sacks of rubbish into the opening at the back. There is no garbage outside Franziska's house.

The church bells ring, eleven o'clock, maybe a few children will be along in half an hour, little ones in fluorescent vests and the older ones with backpacks, some pushing their bicycles up the hill past my car. A little farther up there are two teenagers, a boy and a girl. They are talking, I have watched them for at least ten minutes, before the girl glances down at her watch, makes a horrified and amused face, mutters something, and rapidly stalks off down a side street. The boy watches her a moment too long, then pushes his bike farther up the hill. Is he in love with her? And will he tell her if he is? Will they come together sometime, or lose each other from sight, as life pulls them apart?

During the lunch hour, it's very quiet up here, even the traffic on the through-road has practically ceased. The sun briefly poked through the clouds, causing the wet asphalt to glisten, then the clouds closed up and a little later, it started raining again.

I've eaten nothing since breakfast, but I'm not hungry, I want to pee, but I'm not going to abandon my observation post. Once the automatic light goes on over Franziska's door. It was just a cat, setting off the mechanism, and flouncing off in a huff. I am surprised the light goes on in daytime, perhaps Franziska is worried about burglars? I wonder if the house is alarmed, and with security cameras?

Just before four, a car stops in front of the house, and Anita gets out and skips up the steps. In the lee of the roof, she fishes the key out of her handbag. She hasn't changed much since we were together, basically not since we were at school. She finds the key, unlocks the door, and disappears inside the house.

I hesitate for a long time, but it's my only chance to find out anything about Franziska. I ring the doorbell. Nothing happens. I ring twice more, maybe Anita will open if she thinks it's the mailman or a messenger. And a little later the door opens, and Anita stares out at me. What are you doing here?

I wanted to apologize to Franziska, I say. We... I know, she cuts me off, she told me. She's not here. She starts to shut the door, but seeing me not moving, she opens it again. Do you want to come in then? she asks and sounds much friendlier. Have you been here before? I shake my head and follow her into a bright hallway, which looks amazingly conventional, not to say boring. Would you like some coffee? she asks, and leads me into a large kitchen, which has a view of the garden, the lake below, and the fog-shrouded hills opposite. I'm sure Franziska wouldn't mind you being here. She does really like you, even though you upset her the other day. Where is she? I ask. She had to go away for a couple of days, says Anita evasively.

In the meantime, she's made two cups of coffee with the Nespresso machine and handed me one of them. Seeing as you're here, she says, laughing, you might as well apologize to me too, for not getting in touch again. I'm sorry, I said, the last couple of years were really difficult. Bygones are bygones, says Anita. Would you like a tour of the house?

I wonder what Franziska would think of it, but Anita is determined to show me the house as though it were hers. It's sweet how enthusiastic she is about all of it, here, the four bathrooms, the whirlpool tub, all the kitchen gadgetry and the little soundproofed

studio in the basement. Franziska thought I could
live here while she's away, says Anita, she'd much
rather not leave it empty. But it doesn't feel right
to me. I've only come to water the plants. My
apartment's not bad either. Still in the same place? I
ask. Yes, but my son's moved out. It was about time.
Are you seeing someone? I ask. She shrugs. Are you?
She seems not to expect an answer.

She takes me out into the garden, which is a fair
size. Right beside the house is a walled pool with
tiled surrounds, and behind that a sloping lawn, with
the mighty maple standing to one side. The dark yew
hedge surrounds the entire property, protecting it
from curious eyes, without blocking off its views.

I wouldn't mind the pool, though, says Anita.
Every time I come, I have a quick dip in it. How
about it? It's really not cold. I don't have any trunks
with me. You can't be seen from the street anyway.
Anita is laughing again. I always liked that about her,
how much she laughs, how unencumbered she seems,
without being superficial. Come on! she says. She
undresses.

We stand naked in front of each other. I'm cold,
and it's still spotting with rain. Anita takes me by
the hand, and we slowly climb into the water, which
actually is warmer than the air. We don't stay in for
long, it feels more like a ritual than a proper swim.

I follow Anita out of the water and into the house.
I've rarely felt as naked. Outside the guest bathroom,
Anita suddenly says, no, takes my hand again,
and leads me to Franziska's bathroom. We shower
together, dry off with Franziska's towel, lie in her bed,
in sheets she probably slept in a matter of days ago.
We are both turned on by the idea, though I don't
quite understand why.

Anita has pulled the covers over us, her mouth is
right by my ear. It doesn't matter if you don't love me,
she whispers, it's not your fault. And she's laughing
again. We've both chosen the wrong person, haven't
we? And what do we do now?

When I wake up, it's getting light. I'm all alone
in the bed. I get up and go to the kitchen. Anita is
sitting at the kitchen table, with a cup of tea. I could
use something stronger, I say. Whiskey? Gin? she
asks. I look at my watch. It's five o'clock. Coffee, I say,
and get it myself. Anita is sipping her tea, seems on
the point of saying something, then has another sip.
Damn, that's hot. Where's Franziska? I ask. In the
hospital, she says. She has bad back pains and wanted
to get them checked out. They're afraid it could be to
do with her cancer.

I don't know what to say. For a moment, I feel a kind of savage fury, and am close to hitting Anita or myself, but the fury goes as fast as it came. Perhaps that's why she was a bit sensitive, last time you both spoke, says Anita. Why didn't she say anything, I say quietly. You know what she's like, says Anita. I'm collecting her tomorrow, no, I mean, this afternoon. I hope the doctors have managed to find out what it is.

Anita disappears and comes back soon after with the sheets and the used towel. I need to do the laundry and tidy up a bit, she says. It might be better if you went.

When we say goodbye, it seems to me we're both a little ashamed of what we've done. We mustn't feel ashamed, says Anita, as though she'd read my mind. I'll call you.

Franziska is onstage, singing one of Barbara's songs. Her whole body is trembling with exertion and performance. I am standing offstage, watching. The music stops, she lets her head flop down, the audience applauds. She runs offstage, hugs me, as she would hug anyone standing here. The applause goes on and on, and she has to go back under the lights. I almost can't see her, that's how bright they are.

Night, rain, I'm driving her back to the hotel. The windshield wipers are squeaking. Franziska leans back in her seat, I glance over to her. Her eyes are closed, she looks completely happy, and exhausted.

We're lying in bed, she presses herself against me drowsily, I feel the warmth of her body, smell her hair, her scent, kiss the little hairs on the back of her neck.

We're at the lake, it's rained recently, no one else is around. We get undressed, Franziska has her back to me. When she is naked, she turns toward me, briefly stands there, showing me herself. Then she stoops to pick her bathing suit out of her bag.

We swim in the lake, the sun is low, and the water gleams blackly under it. Franziska dives down, I follow her into the silence. We kiss, I breathe in air she exhales, she breathes in air I exhale. We grow together, we are a single organism, a creature with eight limbs, sinking lower and lower into the depths.

The cardboard folders have to be separated from the paper for recycling, so I take each individual file in my hand to empty it and put contents and folder into separate containers. I remove any paper clips and collect them separately. The archive took so much trouble to build up, now its demolition must be tackled equally painstakingly. Even though I cleaned the basement regularly, the work turns up a lot of dust, and I keep having to take breaks for fresh air. The weather is warmer, but with occasional rain showers. The garden is looking more beautiful than ever, the lilac is blooming, even the peonies are already blooming. It's Franziska's birthday today. In my thoughts I bring her flowers, an enormous bunch of peonies.

Some of the files I browse through before disposing of them. There is no shortage of bland articles, overlap, one journalist cribbing from another. The archive sustained itself, an endless regurgitation of the same, often dubious, facts. But anything once printed becomes truth, acquires authority, and quoting is always allowed. Profiles especially are practically useless, they're so full of holes and have so little to say on what makes someone interesting. Even so, I am tempted to keep the odd file, but I have sworn not to. The archive must be dissolved in its entirety, and removed from my life, the danger of it starting to grow again is simply too great.

In my driveway is a dumpster I ordered, which is now slowly filling up with paper, with photographs and articles. It's possible I'll have to order a second one.

Even though I take my time, I get through the entire archive in under a week. As a message to myself, I have left Franziska's file up in my office, but it too must go. I leaf through it one last time, look at the handful of photographs in which Franziska resembles my recollection of her, a snapshot of an after-concert party, a photo of an awards ceremony, one attached to an interview with a local paper, when she wasn't expecting to be photographed. Strange that she's most herself on the worst photographs. Then, without a further thought, I dump everything in the container with the rest of the papers. The only things I keep are the empty folders that I gave titles to but never filled, The Sound of Water, The Sounds of Birds in Flight, The Smell of Sleep, The Present One, and a few others.

I lie in bed with my eyes shut. I'm not sure whether I'm awake or asleep. I am in town with Franziska, there are a lot of people around, shopping, talking, sitting in outdoor restaurants, strolling around like us, the scene looks like a scale model of a town. We look at each other and are happy. We cross the street and cars stop for us. I thank them with a hand gesture, and I see them all dissolve into thin air, and the motorbikes, mopeds, and bicycles with them. The streetlights vanish, the traffic lights, the road signs. The buildings on either side become

lighter and lighter, until they are invisible, also the
trees and other plants, a front lawn, bushes and
flowers. The dog a woman has on a leash is suddenly
gone; she is left holding the leash. A cat vanishes at
the same time as the birds it was stalking, and finally
the other humans, the passersby, the salespeople,
workmen and waitstaffs, the children disappear
one after the other, as though passing through an
invisible door into a void. Only we two remain,
holding hands, Franziska is laughing, but I don't feel
like laughter. Above us, the clouds melt away, the sky,
the orb of the sun seems to expand until it has taken
over everything in one continuous glare. Then the
ground under our feet is gone, there is nothing left
around us, but we don't fall. Wherever something
existed, there is only a white emptiness left, it feels as
though we are moving on an empty sheet of paper.

In the morning, I am woken by the truck which
picks up my container and takes it away, I hear the
hissing of the hydraulics and the harsh clang of metal
on metal, but I stay in bed, I have no wish to see my
work being disposed of.

I get up late, make my coffee, and go down
into the basement. As I move the empty shelving
aside to create space, a few stray articles come

to light that escaped my purge, a text on the overwintering of cacti, one on the opening of the Gotthard road-tunnel from the eighties, and a new piece on the fiftieth anniversary of Mark Rothko's death, illustrated with a reproduction of one of his paintings. All wind up in the bin. Then I vacuum the basement floor and wipe down the empty shelves. The spatial acoustic is transformed, the roar of the vacuum is strangely loud, and my footfall produces a novel echo.

I feel an overwhelming sense of emptiness; I can't say whether it's positive or negative. It's a mixture of sorrow and lightness, as I've often felt over losses that simultaneously grieved and liberated me.

Now there is only my own story, the file that is my life, and that suddenly seems to me much bigger, much more important now that all the others are gone. What more is there to say?

Anita hasn't gotten in touch again, and I'm not unhappy about that. But ten days after my meeting with her, Franziska calls. I have no idea whether she's been told I was in her house, and what happened there. She doesn't mention it. Nor does she talk about her hospital stay either, all she says is that she hopes our meeting can go ahead sometime.

The weather is improving, and we could sit in the garden. She was always home, I could come whenever I liked, but it had to be this week, because starting on Monday she was embarking on a course of therapy and would prefer not to see anyone. We make a time for the day after tomorrow.

Franziska sounded just as she did during all our recent calls. I don't know what I was expecting. A patient, an invalid, a broken woman? She would never show herself to me like that. Even when I was watching her sleeping, I had the feeling of doing something illicit.

These could be the first days of my life. The archive is gone, the house is clean and tidy. I even toy with the idea of putting it up for sale and leaving. I will see Franziska again after almost thirty years, something old could be finished, something new begin.

When Anita said we had both fallen for the wrong person, my initial response was just to think of Franziska and me. Only now do I start to understand that our relationship was more important to Anita than it was to me. Perhaps she was in love with me all along, as I was with Franziska. Then why did she not say anything? But what difference would it have made? What difference does it make when I tell Franziska I love her, and have always loved her?

———

The next day I go into town to buy new clothes.
I would rather have ordered something online, as
I usually do, but time is short, and I don't want to
appear before Franziska in my old gear. I go along
just after the shops have opened, and I'm in luck, I'm
the only customer. Not even the excessively positive
attitude of the young salesperson can bother me. He
sells me two pairs of pants, three shirts, and a casual
jacket. When I inspect myself in the mirror, I look
to myself as though I'm in disguise, but the young
fellow assures me I look good, and this is what they're
wearing.

On my way home, I happen to pass a hairdresser's
with a couple of empty baby carriages in front of it,
but no one to be seen, no mother and no child. I
decide to get a haircut.

The hairdresser too seems to be in a sunny mood.
She keeps trying to start conversations, but she does
almost all the talking. She tells me about her skiing
holiday in Austria, the time the salon had to be kept
closed, her boyfriend who is also a hairdresser, and
wasn't able to work for two months. Sometimes she felt
stir-crazy in the house, she says, as she washes my hair
and massages my scalp. I could have told him to get

lost. She laughs. She asks me after all those things that constitute a life, what my work is, what my hobbies are, where I live, whether I had kids, where I'd spent my last vacation. All questions I can't answer. I tell her something or other. When she's finally finished, I give her a ridiculously large tip and flee her salon.

My new life hasn't begun yet, and already I'm missing the old one, the even calm of my days, their uneventfulness. The prospect of meeting Franziska makes me anxious, and I ask myself if I'm even up to her ideas of what constitutes a good life? She's bound to want to start giving concerts again, touring, meeting people. Even at school, she never came to rest, always had lots of friends, did sports, made music. I was far from the only person to be in love with her, I was just the one with the most stamina. In retrospect I ask myself what she can have seen in me, what our friendship signified to her. At the time I didn't ask myself that, I was in love and only thought of myself, my wishes and desires. Now I have to confess we would have made an odd couple, the pop singer and the eccentric, beauty and the beast. And it's only in the fairy tale that the beast becomes a prince.

———

Will you come around the outside, I hear Franziska's voice through the entry phone. I'll be right with you.

I walk around the house, and behind the yew hedge find a little gate that leads into the garden, that I failed to remark the other time I was there. The day is sunny, but not warm. The wind tousles the maple leaves. Even before I can sit down at the table, I notice how the cover of the pool is being retracted with a quiet hum. Then Franziska steps out of the house, making an entrance. She is wearing a short summer dress and heels, and strikes me as just as much in disguise as I am. At first glance, she's barely changed at all, but when she steps a little nearer, I can see that the years have left their traces on her. Maybe it's the little wrinkles around her eyes, which no makeup can hide, maybe it's her posture, the way she moves, that betray her age. She smiles as she does in the magazine photographs, performs a strange movement, like a sort of bow, and says, you're looking well, you've hardly changed a bit. That's exactly what I was going to say, I reply, and she laughs. We're probably both pretty well preserved. Would you like a drink?

She disappears inside to get coffee and water, then at last she sits down opposite me, leans back a little, smiles again, but differently, she seems to be more like herself now.

It takes probably half an hour for us to stop speaking in formulae and find our way back to the facility we had on the telephone. Are the marriage proposals still coming? I ask. It's been a while since the last one, she says, I think it's time for another.

It's cooler than we thought, and after a while we move indoors, and the living room table succeeds the garden table; we continue to sit facing one another. We talk about our youth, recollect various exploits, remember old friends and teachers. Do you want something more to drink? she asks, and I'm not sure whether that's a polite suggestion to me to leave. I'm sorry about what I said on the phone, I say. Your relationships are no business of mine. She doesn't reply, just looks at me. I have loved you all my life, I say. Franziska still doesn't speak. She sits there, not moving, like an actress who has forgotten her lines, and isn't sure what to do next. Now I ought to say I still love her, but I'm not sure if that's true, if it's her I love, or my memories of her. She gets up and comes around the table to me. She stops behind my chair, leans down and hugs me, presses her head to mine, without saying anything. Something in me is resistant, but I get up too, and we embrace and kiss.

––––––––

That was lovely, says Fabienne, but I have a
sense something's amiss. I am kneeling between her
legs, looking up at her naked body, she looks much
younger now than before in the garden, uncertain,
vulnerable. Yes, I say, it was lovely. I haven't slept with
anyone in ages, she says, I'm a bit out of practice.
And…She points to the operation scar on her breast
and says nothing further. But that's not what it is.
You're gorgeous, I say, lean over her, kiss her belly,
her breasts, her throat.

We have made love, but it seemed to me as
though it didn't have anything to do with my love, or
with Franziska and me. We were a man and a woman
in a dimly lit room on a puddingy mattress. We
had sex like any couple for the first time. Her hands
and arms, her shoulders, the hollows under her
collarbone, her small breasts and somewhat spreading
hips, liver spots, little hairs, an unexpected pimple,
her smell, the softness of her skin, her pubic hair.
Her way of moving, opening herself, taking what she
wants. Her whispering and laughing, her moaning
and the way she comes, a long moment of absence
and then, still panting, drops onto me, laughs,
whispers something in my ear. That was lovely. Yes, I
say, lovely.

She has turned around; I stroke her back. Have you got sunburn? The skin is reddened on her lower back, a precise rectangle, I am surprised I haven't remarked on it before.

When we were little, there was one manufacturer of sunscreen who used to give out flowers that you could stick on your skin, says Fabienne, do you remember? So that you didn't tan in those places. With me it's the other way around. She turns onto her back again, as though to keep me from seeing it, and I lie next to her. I'm cold, she says, I lost a few pounds in these past months, I don't seem to have a proper appetite anymore.

She pulls the covers over us, then she presses her back against me, and I put my arms around her. We feel closer now than before, when we were making love. I sense she wants to say something, I can feel the thought moving her entire body.

Maybe you rate love between man and woman more highly than I do, she says at last. I was always afraid of your love. I had plans, I wanted to sing, appear in public, be successful. There was no room in that for an unconditional love, which in the end always hurts. The men I was with understood that and allowed me to do what I wanted. I loved them too after my fashion, but I didn't miss them when I was away on tour, and I'm sure they didn't miss me either.

Would you have missed me? I ask. I don't think so, she says, but you would have missed me, and that would have bothered me. I just had the feeling with you, it was all or nothing. And I wasn't able to offer you all. I didn't want to fall in love with you. Do you remember how we were going to go skiing, and instead hung around in my room all day? Or after that concert, we slept in the same bed, wasn't it somewhere in the Black Forest? I think anything might have happened then. But you ran to catch your train, you went into the bathroom to clean your teeth, and you didn't come out for ages. You didn't really want me, you had plans of your own, you were going to study abroad, and publish, become a famous historian or philosopher. What was your thesis going to be about?

What would you do if you could start over? I ask. Fabienne ponders for a long time, then she says, I can't be the one I was once. I don't want to be her either. I think I would do everything the same, just as wrong and just as right. What about you?

I imagine how our life could have been if we had decided differently, if we had come together while we were young. We would have married, had children, Franziska would have worked in the hospital and I in the archive. She would have gone on singing her mournful songs, with maybe the odd appearance at a wedding or a company party in some community center. I would have accompanied her, helped set up and take down the equipment, or else I would have stayed home, minded the kids and waited impatiently for her to come home, always a bit envious of her life without me.

We would have bathed and fed the kids, taken them on vacation, helped them with their homework, driven them to sports practice, comforted them, patched them up.

The children would have grown up and moved out. But had I really wanted these children, had I wanted to share Franziska with them, did I not really want her to be what she was for me all my life, an unattainable love object, a yearning? She had made me happy and unhappy in her absence. Would I have been happier with her there? What would I have had to dream about?

We are walking hand in hand through a forest. The path is broad, the trees make a canopy over us, mighty beeches whose trunks look like pillars of stone. It must be early in the year, the leaves are still a very fresh green. It's cool, but not cold, a breeze is stirring the treetops. A woman on horseback comes down the path toward us, she is sitting terribly upright, her upper body bounces forward and back in time to the horse's trot. Occasional dapples of sun fall through the foliage onto her slim body. Just before she reaches us, she rises in the saddle, and her horse races past us in a gallop.

I can't see Franziska but I can feel her walking at my side, and I hear our steps on the gravel. The light is dazzling, and I turn my head away. We stop. Franziska lets go my hand, I can hear her walking away, but I can't even turn to go after her, an invisible power seems to prevent me.

It's very dark. I can feel the warmth of Fabienne's body. She must have gone to sleep, she mutters and stirs in her sleep, pulling the covers away from me. I have no idea how late it is, how long I've been asleep. I get up and dress, pick up my backpack, and walk through the dark house.

The front door is locked, so I go through the sliding glass doors into the garden to the little garden gate, but that's locked as well. I wonder if I could manage to climb over it. I don't know, and I don't even try, I'd feel too pathetic.

Fabienne must have forgotten to cover over the pool. In the sparse light, the water has an oily black gleam. The trees rustle in the wind. I sit down in one of the poolside deck chairs and look up at the sky. It is clouded over, but there are an astonishing number of stars to be seen; no moon. I am thinking of nothing at all, just sitting there, tired and a little shivery in the chilly night breeze. Dampness seems to rise out of the grass.

Fabienne has come out into the garden. I only notice her when she touches my arm. She spreads a blanket over me and sits down in the deck chair next to mine. She has a blanket for herself too; we must look like a couple of patients at a sanatorium.

Did you think you'd make a break for it, then? she asks. Aren't you a bit old for that? It's a fact, not a question, her voice sounds amused. I knew what I was doing when I locked up.

It's just starting to get light, and the birds are making a huge racket. Did you know that birds with big eyes start singing earlier than birds with smaller eyes? I say. Probably not a lot of people know that, says Fabienne. A good, self-determined life, she says. Are you leading a good, self-determined life? She laughs, without bitterness. I want to get up and give her a hug, but she says, it's all right, stay there. I love you, Fabienne, I say. It's the first time I've tried her name out, and it fits. Let's start over. We've just met tonight. And whom did you meet tonight? she asks. Do you think we can stick it out together? So long as you don't expect too much, I say. You mustn't expect too much either, she says, and tells me about her course of therapy at the hospital, and what she could be in for. I got rid of the archive, I say. Also that I'm thinking about maybe selling the house. I wanted to change my life. You don't have to do that, she says, I'll take you just as you are. I've written it all down, I say. What? Our story? asks Fabienne. No, my story, my file. And how does it end? asks Fabienne. It's not over yet, I say, there's still the closing speech to come. The court doesn't want anything from you, says Fabienne, no one's accusing you except maybe you.

Very gradually it's gotten lighter, the stars have paled and disappeared from view. Do you want to give more concerts? I ask. If I can, says Fabienne, maybe. It's been my life. But right now it doesn't seem all that important. I live from one day to the next, and for all the panic and dread I feel, there's something lovely about it as well.

On the horizon the first peaks catch the sun and take on a fiery red above the low hills and the lake, which are still both in shade. The ones to the left are the Glarner Alps, says Fabienne, the highest of

them is the Mürtschenstock, with its triple summit.
I'm sure you recognize the Vrenelisgärtli, no? And
Tödi is the one all on its own with the wide band
of rock below the summit. I always wanted to climb
it, but probably never will now. The Schärhorn and
the Windgällen. Farther right, the two Mythens, big
and small. The pyramid-shaped Rigi is easy to spot.
Sometimes in the autumn, when the air's very clear,
you can make out Eiger, Mönch, and Jungfrau farther
west. And if you look hard, you may get the sense
that there's more to come, back there.

Peter Stamm is the author of the novels *The Sweet Indifference of the World*, *To the Back of Beyond*, *All Days Are Night*, *Seven Years*, *On a Day Like This*, *Unformed Landscape*, and *Agnes*, and the short-story collections *It's Getting Dark*, *We're Flying*, and *In Strange Gardens and Other Stories*. His award-winning books have been translated into more than thirty languages. For his entire body of work and his accomplishments in fiction, he was short-listed for the Man Booker International Prize in 2013, and in 2014 he won the prestigious Friedrich Hölderlin Prize. He lives in Switzerland.

Michael Hofmann has translated the work of Gottfried Benn, Hans Fallada, Franz Kafka, Joseph Roth, and many others. In 2012 he was awarded the Thornton Wilder Prize for Translation by the American Academy of Arts and Letters. His *One Lark, One Horse: Poems* was published in 2019, *Where Have You Been? Selected Essays* in 2014, and *Selected Poems* in 2009. He lives in Florida and London.